W9-AAD-117

GENERAL MILLS

75 *years of*
innovation invention food **&** fun

GENERAL MILLS

MINNEAPOLIS

Senior Editor: Tom Forsythe

Editor: Anne Brownfield Brown

Design: Yis Vang

Design Assistant: Marie Moreland

Writer: Sarah Huesing

Associate Editor, Historical Research: Katie Dishman

Associate Editor, Production Manager: Judy Hynes

Index: Sandy Laidlaw

Contributors: Josh Burke, Suzanne C. Goodsell, Tess Hohman, Kate Houst, Dori Hummel, Phil Kashian, Penny Leporte, Phil Long, Susan Marks-Kerst, Mike Pearce, Steve Wheeler, Wendy Wortman

Printing: GLS, Minneapolis, Minnesota

Photo Credits:
All images are from the General Mills Archives except those listed here:

Andover Historical Society: Rose and Sarkis Colombosian, p. 13, 62

Marc Norberg Studio, Inc.: Girl with Go-GURT, p. 62

Mike Habermann Photography, Inc.: Baby eating Cheerios, p. 41

Minnesota Historical Society: Interior views of mill, p. 9; Pillsbury A mill, p. 67; WCCO Radio's transmitting station, interior and exterior, p. 75; John Pillsbury Memorial photo, p. 89

New York Stock Exchange Archives: New York Stock Exchange, p. 19

Niedorf Photography: Olive Garden server, p. 86; soccer players, p. 88

General Mills, Minneapolis, Minnesota

© 2003 General Mills
All rights reserved. Published 2003.

ISBN: 0-9746900-0-7

TABLE OF CONTENTS

PROLOGUE

It would be difficult to capture our rich history in a thousand pages. There are simply too many stories to tell.

But this opportunity only comes once – and we couldn't let it pass.

On the 75th anniversary of the creation of General Mills – in our 137th year as a company – we wanted to pause to commemorate at least some of the historical highlights of a great American company.

But where to start? With the creation of General Mills in 1928? Or at the beginning, on the banks of the Mississippi River in 1866? And what of the many companies with which General Mills has been intertwined? What of Pillsbury and Green Giant? What of Kenner and Parker Brothers, Red Lobster and Burger King? What of the products we invented together and the brands we built together?

It was simple really. Pillsbury's history is our history. Green Giant, Old El Paso, Colombo and Häagen-Dazs are here – alive within General Mills. Of the rest we chose to include a little of each, because they too are a part of us. And while we take no credit for the success they enjoy today, we are proud to have shared the same path for at least part of our shared history.

The theme for our celebration? That came easily – because it really has been 75 years of innovation, invention, food and fun.

With a bow to brevity, with apologies for excluding far too many items well-worthy of mention, and with acknowledgment and thanks to the many friends and sources who have helped us prepare these pages, we invite you to join us as we pause to celebrate some of the highlights of our rich and colorful past.

— *Tom Forsythe*

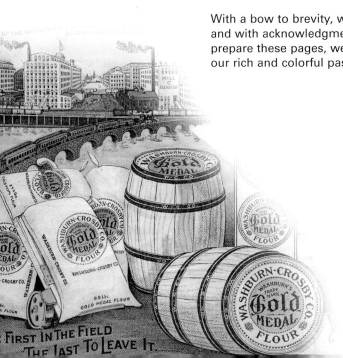

75 years

innovation invention food & fun

*f*rom flour to submarines, from toys to restaurants, General Mills has been making a difference in people's lives for 75 years.

We fully trace our roots to 1866, and to a pair of flour mills on opposite banks of the Mississippi River that would build a city, anchor a region and change the milling industry forever.

Ours is a rich history. Even before our incorporation as General Mills in 1928, our predecessor companies demonstrated a knack for understanding consumers and providing them with innovative and inventive new products.

Our story goes beyond the grocery aisles to the "preppy craze" of alligator shirts and the invention of the "black box." We created advertising icons and secret spy decoder rings. At one point, we were the largest toy maker in the world.

Today, with brands like Cheerios, Pillsbury, Yoplait, Green Giant, Betty Crocker, Old El Paso, Totino's and Progresso, General Mills is still making a difference in consumers' lives.

It's been 75 years of innovation, invention, food and fun – inside and outside the kitchen both in America and around the world.

As we celebrate, let's look at 75 highlights.

innovation invention food & fun

innovation

A blast from the past

The puffing gun, developed in the late 1930s by General Mills engineer and chemist Thomas R. James, allowed the company to expand or "puff" pellets into different cereal shapes. It was the crucial technology component in the development of Kix cereal in 1937, and would be used to create Cheerioats in 1941.

Tak Tsuchiya, a General Mills engineer, improved on James' invention with an innovation that allowed the puffing gun to puff cereal continually, instead of in batches. He worked on the upgrade for nearly six years, and introduced it to General Mills manufacturing facilities in 1960. The continuous cereal puffing gun not only puffed a greater volume of cereal, but produced a more uniform product and reduced quality control losses from 10 percent of production to less than 3 percent.

In 1956, the Strato-Lab balloon, developed by General Mills' Aeronautical Research Labs, reached a record height of 76,000 feet. Two General Mills engineers still hold the record for vertical ascent in an unpressurized balloon gondola.

In 1957, General Mills began producing recipes on records for people who couldn't use a traditional cookbook. Made of light and unbreakable material, the records provided instructions relevant to a person without sight. Adelaide Hawley, who portrayed Betty Crocker on television, provided the voice.

In 1924, the *Betty Crocker Cooking School of the Air* debuted. It was first broadcast on the Washburn Crosby Company's own radio station, WCCO.

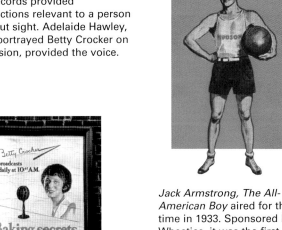

Jack Armstrong, The All-American Boy aired for the first time in 1933. Sponsored by Wheaties, it was the first juvenile adventure radio serial. Highly popular, *Jack Armstrong* ran on radio until 1951.

The curiosity of a General Mills sales executive led to the creation of a new baking mix category with the development of Bisquick. When served fresh biscuits on a train, the salesman questioned the chef on how he could have mixed and baked fresh biscuits so quickly. The chef showed the salesman his special mixture, and the salesman brought the idea to a company chemist, who worked to develop the unique baking mix. Introduced in 1931, Bisquick became so popular that within months, there were nearly 100 competing biscuit mixes on the market.

Green Giant created a new category of prepared meal dinner solutions when Create a Meal! was launched in 1993. With frozen vegetables and sauce in one bag, the meals brought a new level of convenience to busy kitchens everywhere.

Marketing innovations that sing and swing

For six years, the Wheaties Quartet harmonized about the benefits of Wheaties with its song "Have You Tried Wheaties?" Believed to be the first singing radio commercial, the song was first aired on Christmas Eve 1926. Local Wheaties sales improved dramatically, and the commercial was aired nationally in 1929.

Many athletes have endorsed Wheaties through the years, including Lou Gehrig, Joe DiMaggio, Jackie Robinson, Bob Feller, Hank Greenberg, Stan Musial, Ted Williams, Yogi Berra, Mickey Mantle, Johnny Bench and Babe Ruth, the sultan of swat.

Wheaties sponsored the first televised commercial sports broadcast in 1939. The game between the Cincinnati Reds and the Brooklyn Dodgers was aired on NBC to a small audience – the roughly 500 owners of television sets in New York City.

innovation invention food & fun

The debut of Go-GURT in 1999 was revolutionary. The yogurt-in-a-tube packaging concept was an immediate hit with kids and parents across the United States.

General Mills developed the package tear strip in 1956, making it easier for consumers to open a variety of everyday food products.

The "Breakfast of Champions" slogan was first used in 1933 on a signboard on the left-field wall of old Nicollet Park in Minneapolis, the home of the minor-league Minneapolis Millers. It would become one of the most venerable slogans in advertising history.

In 1983, Eddie Bauer formed an innovative cross-branding partnership with Ford. The first "Eddie Bauer Bronco" appeared on America's roads in 1984 as a limited edition. General Mills owned Eddie Bauer from 1971 to 1988.

Green Giant launched "boil-in-bag" vegetables in 1961. This innovation created a convenient new way to prepare vegetables.

After years of holding regional shareholder meetings, General Mills decided to try something new. On October 29, 1959, the company connected stockholders across the country in one meeting via closed-circuit television. General Mills executives presided at each location, and two-way communication was maintained throughout. It was the first nationwide closed-circuit meeting.

In 1955, General Mills began the Betty Crocker Search for the All-American Homemaker of Tomorrow. When the program ended in 1977, more than 9.5 million high school seniors had taken part, and General Mills had awarded more than $2.1 million in student scholarships.

Depths of innovation

General Mills was awarded a contract by the U.S. Navy and the Woods Hole Oceanographic Institute to develop a small, deep-diving submarine in 1962.

Harold "Bud" Froehlich of General Mills' Aeronautical Research Labs drafted the first design for the 15-foot submarine. Within a couple years, the submarine – nicknamed ALVIN after Allyn Vine of the Woods Hole Oceanographic Institute – was deployed.

Since 1964, ALVIN has been part of many important expeditions, including the first dives to the Titanic in 1986 and the recovery of a hydrogen bomb from the ocean floor. ALVIN is still operating and in use today.

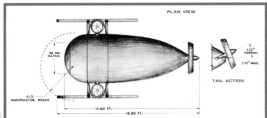

Fish, fries and apple pies

Pillsbury began testing the Poppin Fresh Pie Shop restaurant concept in Des Moines, Iowa, in 1970. The idea was a success, and within years, all of America could enjoy all-American apple pie.

Red Lobster expanded quickly after being purchased by General Mills in 1970, bringing fresh seafood from the coasts to the heartland. From a three-restaurant chain, General Mills added 350 restaurants in under 10 years.

General Mills developed a new restaurant concept in 1982. One of the first national Italian chains, The Olive Garden opened 50 new restaurants each year at its peak, bringing a bit of Tuscany and "Hospitaliano" to family dining.

Burger King, acquired by Pillsbury in 1967, launched its "Have It Your Way" advertising campaign in 1974. For the first time, fast-food consumers could have burgers made to order, providing a major area of distinction for Burger King.

innovation invention food & fun

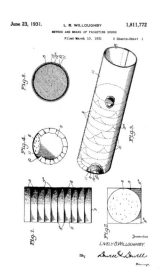

Thomas R. James, a chemist and engineer, designed the first version of the James Cooker – a cooker and extruder that makes round pellets of dough. An evolved version of the James Cooker is still used today to make many General Mills cereals.

Howard Bauman, a Pillsbury food safety expert, developed the Hazard Analysis and Critical Control Point (HACCP) process in 1971 to ensure food safety. HACCP is now a food industry standard and is used by the U.S. Food and Drug Administration.

In 1925, the Minnesota Valley Canning Company developed the seeds for a larger, more tender pea. The new larger size peas were dubbed "Green Giant" – a name that would eventually become known around the world.

U.S. Patent   Oct. 28, 1980   Sheet 1 of 2   4,230,924

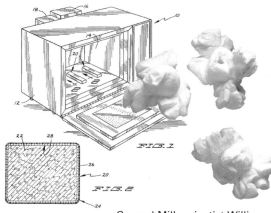

The patent of the Willoughby can in 1931 gave the Ballard & Ballard Company sole rights to a unique new method of packaging unbaked dough. Named after its inventor, Lively B. Willoughby, the important technology was acquired by Pillsbury as part of its acquisition of Ballard & Ballard in 1951.

The Bellera "Air Spun" process for milling flour was developed by General Mills in 1960. The new process was less costly and faster than older methods because it drastically reduced the amount of handling and the number of steps necessary to turn wheat into flour.

In 1934, the Minnesota Valley Canning Company (later renamed the Green Giant Company) developed the "heat unit theory" to determine crop maturity and ensure that vegetables are delivered to canneries at the peak of flavor.

General Mills scientist William Brastad helped discover a new application for metallized polyester in the late 1970s. The technology was later used to develop the packaging for microwave popcorn.

Blue sky technology

In the winter of 1953, the General Mills Mechanical division worked in conjunction with the University of Minnesota to develop technology that forever changed the way airplane flight data is recorded. The Ryan flight recorder evolved into the "black box" found today in every commercial airliner – one of the most important tools in airline disaster investigations.

Usually located in the tail of the airplane, the "black box" captures an exact record of the airplane's air speed, altitude, vertical acceleration, elapsed time, flight duration and weather effects. James Ryan, the University of Minnesota professor for whom it is named, designed the box to continue functioning for at least five minutes after the plane's loss of power and to protect the stored information for more than 30 minutes after being exposed to flames of 1,000 degrees Fahrenheit.

"The extreme cost of air failure in terms of human lives and demolished equipment worth millions of dollars makes it important to constantly measure the atmospheric conditions surrounding the aircraft," said Ryan in 1953. "Eliminating the cause of just one crash would make the instrument worthwhile."

Milling milestones

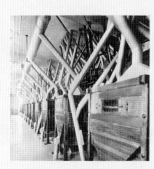

To make grayish spring wheat flour more appealingly white, Cadwallader Washburn installed the revolutionary middlings purifier in his mill in the 1870s.

In 1879, Cadwallader Washburn installed a new steel roller milling system in his C mill on an experimental basis to demonstrate the value of rollers compared to millstones. It was the first complete automatic roller mill in the world.

In 1939, General Mills engineer Helmer Anderson created the Anderson sealer. By allowing flour packages to be closed with glue instead of tied with a string, the machine revolutionized packaging and sealing.

innovation invention food & fun

Ho ho ho!

Originally created to describe a new, larger pea developed by the Minnesota Valley Canning Company in 1925, Green Giant would come to define the company. The Green Giant character first appeared in advertising in 1928, and through the years the Giant became so popular that the company formally changed its name to the Green Giant Company in 1950.

General Mills created Total cereal in 1961. Total was the first cereal to contain 100 percent of the minimum daily adult requirement for eight vitamins, as recommended by the U.S. government, representing a major advance in cereal vitamin fortification.

Hamburger Helper dinner mix launched nationally in 1971 in an era of rising meat prices. The five varieties were marketed as convenient and economical meal "helpers" for the cook of the family, creating an entirely new grocery category. The Helper line grew quickly and, in 1972, Tuna Helper was introduced.

Cheerioats debuted as the company's third cereal in 1941. It was the country's first ready-to-eat oat cereal. Four years later, to settle a trademark dispute with a competitor, Cheerioats changed its name to Cheerios, proving quite fortuitous. Today, Cheerios is the No. 1 selling cereal brand in America.

Kix cereal was introduced in 1937. It was General Mills' second breakfast cereal and the first ready-to-eat puffed corn cereal.

In 1966, Ella Rita Hefrich was named a winner at the Pillsbury Bake-Off Contest for her Tunnel of Fudge cake recipe. The cake was prepared in a special bundt pan, and the recipe became so popular that Pillsbury introduced Bundt cake mix in 1972.

Old El Paso introduced Mexican food to consumers from Scandinavia to Australia. Pillsbury acquired the Old El Paso brand in 1995 with the acquisition of Pet, Inc.

Bugles, the first cone-shaped corn snack, was launched nationally in 1966, and every Bugle-eating kid since has done this at least once. Daisy*s, Buttons, Bows and Whistles would follow, not to toot any horns.

First ladies of flour

Ann Pillsbury

Ann Pillsbury's signature was a sign of quality for Pillsbury baking products. She had her own test kitchen and recipes. Created in 1944, Ann Pillsbury's signature is all we have of her today – there was never a portrait of her that we know of.

Martha Meade

Martha Meade was the face of flour on the West Coast. Created by the Sperry Flour Company – as a (mythical) contemporary of Betty Crocker – her recipes and cookbooks were published for years, and she also was on radio.

The "Betty Crocker of the South," Martha White was the only one of our "first ladies" who was actually a real person. Martha White Lindsay was the daughter of Richard Lindsay, Sr., founder of the Royal Flour Mill in Nashville, Tennessee. The name of the company changed to Martha White, the mill's most popular brand, in 1941. General Mills divested the Martha White brand in 2001.

Betty Crocker

Betty Crocker was created in 1921 as a pen name to personalize responses to the company's consumer inquiries about Gold Medal flour. She was so popular that in 1945 Betty Crocker was the second most recognizable female in the country after Eleanor Roosevelt.

innovation invention food & fun

Out of this world

When NASA astronaut Scott Carpenter launched into space on Aurora 7 in 1962, he was carrying with him the first solid space food – small food cubes developed by Pillsbury's research and development department.

Taking Pillsbury scientists more than a year to develop, space food cubes were followed by other space-friendly foods, such as non-crumbly cake, relish that could be served in slices and meat that needed no refrigeration. From the efforts to feed our astronauts came the popular land-based Space Food Sticks.

Space Food Sticks were an instant hit when they landed in the grocery aisle in 1969. They had the same nutritional value as the food developed for NASA, but for the astronauts of the future they came in appealing flavors: chocolate, caramel and peanut butter.

Fruit you can roll up and put in your pocket was popular from the start. Four Fruit Roll-Ups fruit snack flavors were introduced in 1979, combining consumers' desire to snack with the nutritious value of fruit. They were rolled out nationally in 1983. New Fruit Roll-Ups flavors and varieties were added soon after.

The first Betty Crocker packaged cake mix came in 1947. Ginger Cake, the first flavor, was followed by Party Cake and Devil's Food Cake mixes two years later.

OvenReady biscuits were only a regional product when Pillsbury acquired Ballard & Ballard in 1951. But the patented process held great promise. Today, over two billion refrigerated biscuits, rolls and breads are sold each year – now that's a lot of lovin' from the oven!

General Mills used fluorescent lighting technology to quickly grow Bibb lettuce and other salad greens indoors after buying the Phytofarm patent and hiring its inventor Noel Davis in 1974. The greens were sold commercially, but discontinued in 1982 because of high production costs.

Rolling along

After nearly a decade of development incorporating specialized dough formulation and innovative technology, Pillsbury refrigerated pie crusts were released nationally in 1983.

Colombo was America's first yogurt company, introducing yogurt to the United States. In 1929, Rose Colombosian began making yogurt in her kitchen based on a family recipe brought from Armenia. At that time, most consumers in the United States were unfamiliar with yogurt. General Mills bought Colombo in 1993.

Pillsbury launched Toaster Strudel in 1985. Although it took six years of development and testing, the new frozen breakfast pastry was a big success.

Pillsbury introduced its Shape cookies in 1992. The first cookies featured teddy bears and dinosaurs, although their popularity quickly led to holiday-themed cookies.

World War II was the impetus for flour enrichment. When the government mandated flour enrichment to improve the health of Americans, General Mills was already on the forefront of research and began adding vitamins and iron to Gold Medal and its other flours.

Slice 'n Bake cookie dough was introduced by Pillsbury in 1957. It was a convenient new way to bake fresh hot cookies.

innovation invention food & fun

Of moose and men

Bullwinkle, the lovable cartoon moose, and his loyal sidekick Rocky, the flying squirrel, are just two of the famous cartoon characters associated with General Mills and its products. The company sponsored the television show *Rocky and His Friends* beginning in 1959. *The Bullwinkle Show* began in 1961.

Produced by Jay Ward, the creator of Rocky and Bullwinkle, the shows also gave rise to a daily comic strip featuring the moose and squirrel and their cohorts in 1962.

The famous pair were featured in numerous television and print advertisements and on cereal packages for General Mills until 1968.

In 1977, Kenner Products, a General Mills subsidiary, purchased the "galaxy-wide" toy rights to the name and images for the *Star Wars* movies. Demand for *Star Wars* toys quickly outstripped supply, and Kenner actually sold certificates of ownership until more toys could be produced. In their first year, the *Star Wars* toys generated approximately $100 million in revenue.

"Baby Alive" – the doll from Kenner that "eats and drinks and feels soft like a real baby" – was launched for the 1973 holiday season.

"Monster Cereals" were introduced by General Mills in the 1970s, including Count Chocula, Franken Berry and Boo Berry. Two other Monster Cereals, Fruit Brute and Yummy Mummy, were discontinued in the late 1980s.

Foot-Joy, then part of General Mills' Fashion division, introduced the Sta-Sof cabretta leather golf glove in 1980. It quickly became the No. 1 selling golf glove, one almost every golfer has owned at one time.

A new "super hero," Stretch Armstrong was introduced to the world by Kenner in 1976. Stretch's amazing ability to "stretch and stretch" then snap back to his original shape made him a phenomenon. Finding exactly how Stretch was able to stretch and snap back was irresistible to many – often leading to Stretch's demise.

In 1970, General Mills' Parker Brothers subsidiary released Nerf products. It was the first time Parker Brothers strayed from family games, but Nerf became an instant hit, with more than four million Nerf balls sold the first year.

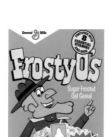

Dudley Do-Right, the Canadian Mountie, always got his man. Persistently pursuing Snidely Whiplash and regularly rescuing his girlfriend Nell, Dudley appeared on *The Bullwinkle Show*, and on General Mills' Frosty O's cereal.

The giggle that launched a thousand chips

One of the world's best-loved advertising icons, Poppin' Fresh, the Pillsbury Doughboy, made his first television appearance in 1965. The venerable Doughboy was created with the help of the Leo Burnett advertising agency, and within three years was recognized by 87 percent of American consumers.

The Doughboy remains fresh and wholesome, speaking nearly a dozen languages and still blushing easily.

innovation invention food & fun

fun

Best Wishes The Lone Ranger & Tonto

Who was that masked man?

For two decades, General Mills brought radio listeners, then television viewers, the adventures of *The Lone Ranger*. General Mills' long-running sponsorship began with the radio show in 1941 and ended 20 years later with *The Lone Ranger* television show in 1961. During that time, the Lone Ranger, his horse Silver, and his faithful companion Tonto appeared on scores of cereal packages.

General Mills created countless Lone Ranger-related premiums that appeared on Wheaties, Kix and Cheerios boxes, some of which were announced only during the radio show. The largest and most popular may have been the Lone Ranger frontier town.

The frontier town premium came in four sections and, when assembled, depicted an entire western town on a 4.5-square-foot sheet. Each section cost 10 cents and one Cheerios box top. Once together, children could add extra buildings found on the back of Cheerios boxes. For an entire year, radio listeners could follow the adventures of the Lone Ranger and his horse in the frontier town.

To celebrate the Cheerios 60th anniversary in 2001, General Mills released a special commemorative Lone Ranger cereal package. The Cheerios box was a replica of one that first appeared in 1948 and was banded with the 60th anniversary Cheerios box.

Toying around

General Mills' first toy company acquisition was the 1965 purchase of Cincinnati-based Rainbow Crafts, maker of Play-Doh modeling compound. General Mills tinkered with the product's formula, reduced production costs and tripled the subsidiary's revenue in about three years.

Totino's founders, Rose Totino and her husband Jim, began their business with a $50,000 loan and the family pizza recipe. Pillsbury purchased Totino's in 1975. Totino's reached a milestone in 1994, producing one million pizzas a day on average.

General Mills' Izod and Lacoste clothing brands were at the center of the preppie craze that erupted in the 1970s. If you didn't have an alligator on your polo shirt, you simply weren't in style.

The Betty Crocker Kitchens have their roots in the test kitchens of the Washburn Crosby Company. The kitchens were formally named the Betty Crocker Kitchens in 1946, and they moved to their current location at the General Mills headquarters in Golden Valley, Minnesota, in 1958. Nearly two million people visited the Betty Crocker Kitchens on tours offered from 1958 to 1985, making them one of the state's top tourist attractions.

Kenner Products introduced children to the world of baking with the Kenner Easy Bake Oven in 1963. With General Mills' purchase of Kenner Toys in 1967, it became known as the Betty Crocker Easy Bake Oven.

General Mills acquired the rights to what is perhaps America's greatest board game – Monopoly – when it purchased Parker Brothers in 1968. Created by Charles Darrow (above), the game was introduced during the Great Depression. Monopoly is still one of America's top-selling games.

The Spirograph toy, introduced by Kenner in 1966, was an immediate success and spawned spinoffs such as Spirotot, Cyclograph and Spiroman.

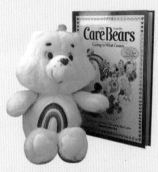

General Mills' Toy division developed Care Bears in conjunction with American Greetings in 1983. Care Bears followed on the Toy division's success with the Strawberry Shortcake doll, originally released in 1981.

A memory maker, General Mills' Lionel trains brightened countless gift occasions. General Mills acquired the rights to manufacture and sell Lionel products under license in 1970.

GIS: *taking stock in the future*

James Ford Bell is rightly viewed as the founder of General Mills. But if not for a lone dissenter on the board of a still-unknown company that had offered to purchase the Washburn Crosby Company in 1928, General Mills may never have come to be.

Washburn Crosby had accepted the purchase offer, and the contracts were nearly signed when the purchasing company abruptly withdrew. Knowing that a dramatic moment was at hand, Bell instead went across the street to a New York investment banker and advanced a plan for a horizontal integration of milling companies. By June 1928, Bell had aligned four other milling companies to merge into the new General Mills. Red Star Milling Company, Royal Milling Company, Kalispell Flour Mills Company, and Rocky Mountain Elevator Company joined the Washburn Crosby Company to create one of the largest milling companies in the world.

General Mills came into existence on June 22, 1928, two days after its incorporation. The new company's broad-minded philosophy of allowing mills to maintain their own identities impressed bankers, and Washburn Crosby's track record impressed the American public. In Chicago, the allotment of stock to brokers was sold before a formal selling campaign could even commence.

First Annual Report
OF
GENERAL MILLS, INC.

June 1, 1928,
to
May 31, 1929

July 25, 1929

At its first official board meeting in June 1928, the new board of directors issued GIS stock to acquire the assets of the five companies, with the stock indicating the value of each company within General Mills: 135,418 shares to the Washburn Crosby Company; 20,152 to the Red Star Milling Company; 8,122 to the Royal Milling Company; 3,671 to the Kalispell Flour Mills Company; and 2,637 to the Rocky Mountain Elevator Company.

Although little had been added physically to what the Washburn Crosby Company owned before the merger, investors believed the new company would grow more quickly than if the various mills had remained independent. That confidence was reflected in General Mills' stock price, which was issued at $65, but quickly rose to $86. The stock first traded as GIS on the New York Stock Exchange on November 30, 1928.

GENERAL MILLS paid a dividend of $1.10 per share for fiscal 2003. The company and its predecessor firm have paid shareholder dividends without interruption or reduction for 105 years.

Merging mills

At its core, General Mills was a flour milling company. For more than 130 years, General Mills and its predecessor companies have provided consumers across the nation and around the world with top-quality flour. In fact, Gold Medal flour has been a top-selling flour in the United States since its debut in 1880.

The Sperry Flour Company's Drifted Snow flour was the most prominent flour brand on the West Coast when Sperry was incorporated into General Mills in 1929. Sperry's other flours included La Bandera, Harina and Gold Seal flour.

Sperry's La Piña flour was introduced in 1910. Formulated from soft wheat specifically for use in tortillas and other Mexican dishes, La Piña is still a popular brand in the Southwest, though General Mills sold the La Piña brand when it acquired Pillsbury in 2001.

The Red Star Milling Company contributed the Red Star Perfect Process, Red Star Enriched and Vitalife flour brands to the company. Kalispell Flour Mills Company's SunDown Bleached and Fluffy White brands, as well as the Rex flours from the Royal Milling Company also became part of General Mills in 1928.

General Mills purchased Red Band Company, Inc. in 1933, along with its Red Band flour brand, a multipurpose soft wheat flour milled specifically for use in quick breads, biscuits and cakes. Red Band also was sold in 2001.

Many different flour brands have dotted the history of General Mills, but the most well-known remains Gold Medal flour – still the leading consumer flour brand in America.

Flour power

In the last century, no flour advertising campaign was as well known as the "Eventually ... Why Not Now?" campaign created by the Washburn Crosby Company.

Very few advertising slogans last for decades. But then, very few are like "Eventually ... Why Not Now?" Created in 1907 by Benjamin S. Bull, advertising manager for the Washburn Crosby Company, the slogan lasted well into the 1940s.

Although many different stories exist as to how Bull created the famous words, the most likely is that Bull was given a long list of reasons people should use Gold Medal flour. Each point was preceded with the word "eventually." Bull took a pencil and slashed through most of the words, writing "Eventually – why not now?" He then threw the paper in the wastebasket. The president's son, James Ford Bell, retrieved the paper and encouraged Bull to use it.

The company spent $650,000 on the "Eventually" campaign – an astronomical amount in the early 1900s, but it paid off handsomely in popularity and longevity. The phrase became so popular, it was quickly picked up

by other businesses worldwide, who modified it for their own uses – advertising everything from Harley-Davidson motorcycles to banking services.

Even then-competitor Pillsbury used the "Eventually" slogan to their advantage by seemingly posting an answer. Next to a Washburn Crosby Company billboard advertising "Eventually ... Why Not Now?" Pillsbury created its own billboard stating "Because Pillsbury's Best."

Pillsbury's Best flour broke milling protocol when it created its familiar barrelhead logo with four "X"s. At that time, millers used three "X"s to distinguish between flour qualities. If flour was marked with three "X"s, it was the miller's highest quality flour. By adding another "X," Pillsbury set its flour apart, indicating it was superior to the other leading flours on the market. In 1872, Pillsbury's Best trademark name and four-"X" logo were registered.

In 1923, the Washburn Crosby Company implemented a new advertising program for its flour. A surplus of wheat and a dwindling world market was driving down prices for farmers. In the interest of public good, Washburn Crosby initiated a new campaign, adding the slogan "Eat More Wheat" to all of its ads. The American Bakers Association endorsed the idea, as did many other grocery and farming organizations. Other companies also began using the slogan, including Pillsbury. Although the campaign lasted a short time, the phrase became ubiquitous in many parts of the country in the mid-1920s.

The first lady of food

When Betty Crocker was not quite 25 years old, she was voted the second most recognizable female in the United States, after Eleanor Roosevelt. Today, Betty Crocker is more than 80, but she is still one of the most recognizable names in the kitchen. At the height of her popularity, Betty Crocker received as many as 5,000 letters every day. What's more amazing is that she answered nearly every one – quite impressive for a woman who is technically a portrait.

In 1921, a simple advertisement ran in the *Saturday Evening Post* magazine. The ad, for Gold Medal flour, asked consumers to complete and return a jigsaw puzzle to receive a small pin cushion. Along with some 30,000 completed puzzles came several hundred letters asking various cooking- and baking-related questions.

In a stroke of marketing genius, the advertising department convinced executives to create a female personality within Washburn Crosby Company's Home Service department to reply to the questions. The surname Crocker was chosen in honor of a recently retired director, William G. Crocker, and "Betty" was chosen simply because of its friendly sound.

1936

1955

1972

1980

Betty Crocker

1965

1968

1986

1996

An informal contest between female employees of the department was held to find the most distinctive Betty Crocker signature. Florence Lindberg's version was chosen, and it remains the basis of the Betty Crocker signature of today.

Officially, Betty Crocker didn't receive a face until Neysa McMein, a prominent commercial artist, was commissioned to create a portrait in 1936. McMein's rendition, with a classic red jacket and white collar, established a tradition for future portraits and remained the official likeness for nearly 20 years.

In 1955, six well-known artists, including Norman Rockwell, were invited to paint fresh interpretations of Betty Crocker. About 1,600 women from across the country evaluated the finished works and chose the portrait by illustrator Hilda Taylor – a softer, smiling version of the original image.

Remaining contemporary with changing consumers, Betty Crocker updated her image six more times over the years – most recently in 1996, for her 75th birthday. A computerized composite of 75 women who embodied the characteristics of Betty Crocker, along with the 1986 portrait, served as inspiration for the painting. The portrait, by internationally known artist John Stuart Ingle, was unveiled March 19, 1996, in New York City.

John Stuart Ingle creates the 1996 portrait of Betty Crocker.

Stirring up excitement

Betty Crocker received a voice in 1924 with the launch of the *Gold Medal Flour Home Service Talks* on the Washburn Crosby Company's WCCO radio station. The *Betty Crocker Cooking School of the Air* soon followed.

Blanche Ingersoll provided the voice for Betty Crocker initially. Every Friday morning, Ingersoll would broadcast recipes, baking ideas and household tips. Listeners "enrolled" in the school by requesting recipes. The "homework" was making the recipes and writing a report. Those who completed all recipes and lessons graduated during a broadcast ceremony. One of the first radio shows dedicated to homemakers, the Betty Crocker cooking school was a huge hit, with more than 200 "graduates" in the first class.

The show expanded to 13 markets – each regional Betty Crocker had a different voice, but they all read scripts prepared by the Home Service department in Minneapolis.

Through its various incarnations over 27 years on the air, the *Betty Crocker Cooking School of the Air* remains one of the longest-running shows in radio history.

As the show grew in popularity, expanding into even more markets, so did the fame of Betty Crocker. At the height of her popularity, Betty Crocker was receiving 5,000 letters a day. Most letters requested cooking advice or recipes, but Betty Crocker also received more unusual requests – including marriage proposals. As Betty Crocker was married to her work, she had to decline all proposals.

The Betty Crocker personality is so engaging that even today some people still believe she is a real person.

A coupon in Gold Medal flour for a free Wm. Rogers & Son teaspoon in 1931 was an overwhelming success, launching one of the longest-running consumer promotions ever.

One year after that promotion, General Mills created a program where consumers could save and redeem multiple coupons to receive entire sets of flatware. Oneida replaced Wm. Rogers & Son in 1936, as the Betty Crocker coupon program continued to grow, until at one point, General Mills was the largest distributor of Oneida's Community patterns of stainless steel flatware in the nation. Available in four patterns, the Community style was designed especially for Betty Crocker coupon savers.

Suspended during World War II, the promotion resumed in 1947. By 1962, the program had grown well beyond flatwear, with publication of the first Betty Crocker coupon catalog.

To avoid confusion with cents-off coupons, the program was renamed "Betty Crocker Catalog Points" in 1992. Today, consumers can purchase items from the Betty Crocker catalog with cash and points.

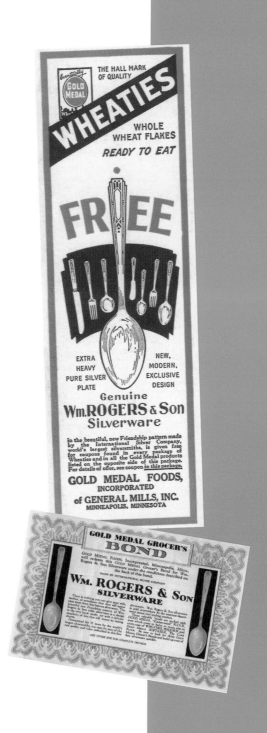

What's cooking?

Although the Betty Crocker Kitchens have evolved through the years, they still remain state-of-the-art. What would become the Betty Crocker Kitchens actually began as Washburn Crosby's test kitchens inside the A mill. Those kitchens, created before the birth of Betty Crocker, were full of modern conveniences like running water and gas stoves.

Those orginal kitchens would evolve into the General Mills test kitchens where staff would not only conduct cooking and baking tests, but also answer consumer letters, compile recipes, produce the material for the Betty Crocker radio shows, and host informal tours.

The kitchens formally changed their name to the "Betty Crocker Kitchens" in 1946. To accommodate the large numbers of visitors, General Mills began a daily tour schedule when its kitchens opened at its new headquarters in 1958 in Golden Valley, Minnesota. Invitations were sent, inviting people to "Come into our kitchens and see how we test and develop recipes, work on new products and perfect quicker, easier methods to help you in your homemaking."

In 1985, General Mills closed its kitchens to the public, in part to preserve the confidentiality of General Mills' new product research. At the time, five of

THE PENNSYLVANIA DUTCH KITCHEN

THE HAWAIIAN KITCHEN

THE CAPE COD KITCHEN

the seven kitchens had already been closed to the public to maintain the secrecy of new product development and testing.

During the years the kitchens were open, millions visited to catch a glimpse of where Betty Crocker created her famous recipes. Everyone from elementary school students to politicians and celebrities were drawn to Betty Crocker and her cooking.

Betty Crocker got a brand new kitchen in 2003. Her new 13,595-square-foot facility includes 22 microwaves, 18 refrigerators and 15 freezers. In this space, Betty Crocker Kitchens home economists are fully equipped to create delicious recipes for a whole new generation of cooks.

Recipes for success

From apple pie to pad Thai, Betty Crocker and Pillsbury have helped create family favorites for more than a century with thousands of delicious recipes.

General Mills' cookbook ventures began in 1903 with the *Gold Medal Flour Cook Book*. The first *Betty Crocker Picture Cook Book* was published in 1950. Dubbed "Big Red," it quickly became one of the best-selling books in the country, and was second in sales only to the Bible for a time.

Pillsbury issued its first cookbook, *A Book for a Cook*, in 1905. The popular *Pillsbury Family Cookbook* made its debut in 1963.

Many specialty cookbooks have been created, such as *Betty Crocker's Living with Cancer Cookbook.* Also popular are Pillsbury and Betty Crocker recipe magazines. Pillsbury published its first recipe magazine in 1949 to share the winning recipes from its inaugural Bake-Off Contest. General Mills published its first recipe magazine, *Creative Recipes with Bisquick*, in 1981.

Through 2002, nearly 200 million Pillsbury and Betty Crocker recipe magazines have been welcomed into consumers' kitchens.

And the winner is...

In 1949, Pillsbury held its first "Grand National Recipe and Baking Contest." The company's advertising agency created the contest in celebration of Pillsbury's 80th birthday. It was quickly dubbed the "Bake-Off," and thousands of recipes were sent in.

The company chose 100 finalists, including three men, to go to New York and prepare their recipes. The first grand prize winner was Theodora Smafield of Michigan who won $50,000 for her yeast-bread recipe for No-Knead Water-Rising Twists.

The contest was such a success that Pillsbury decided to make it a tradition, adapting "Bake-Off Contest" as the official name. After the first year, a junior division was added.

Many popular recipes from the last 50 years have their origin in the Bake-Off Contest. In 1954, sesame seeds were virtually out of stock in supermarkets because of Dorothy Koteen's winning recipe for Open Sesame Pie. When Tunnel of Fudge Cake made its appearance in the 1966 winners' circle, Pillsbury received thousands of requests for help in locating the ring-shaped Bundt cake pan used in the recipe.

The first million-dollar Bake-Off Contest prize went to Kurt Wait of California, for his Macadamia Fudge Torte in 1996.

From Pillsbury's $100,000
GRAND NATIONAL
Recipe and Baking Contest

100
Prize-Winning
Recipes

Have you tried Wheaties?

Like many great inventions, Wheaties cereal was discovered almost by accident. In 1921, a health clinician in Minneapolis spilled bran gruel mix on a hot stove. The gruel baked into a crispy flake. Upon tasting his new creation, he decided it had promise.

The flakes were brought to researchers at the Washburn Crosby Company where the head miller, George Cormack, set about perfecting the product. His top priority was making the flakes stronger so they didn't turn to dust in the box. After testing more than 35 formulas, Cormack finally found the perfect flake.

Jane Bausman, the wife of a General Mills export manager, won the companywide naming contest for the new product. Her idea, "Wheaties," was chosen over entries such as Nutties and the original name, Gold Medal Whole Wheat Flakes.

With sales lagging in 1929, General Mills considered discontinuing the product when advertising manager Sam Gale noticed that the majority of Wheaties customers

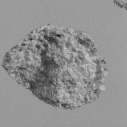

were in regions where they could hear the Wheaties Quartet. General Mills had introduced the Wheaties Quartet to radio listeners in Minneapolis in 1926. Its catchy tune "Have You Tried Wheaties?" helped boost sales tremendously in the listening area with what is believed to be the first singing advertisement on radio. Gale urged the company to take the commercial national. It did – and Wheaties sales soared.

In 1933, nine years after the cereal was introduced, Gale and legendary ad man Knox Reeves coined what would become one of the most famous advertising slogans in history – "The Breakfast of Champions."

Gale was also the innovator behind the idea of sponsoring radio broadcasts of local baseball games. General Mills' contract for the broadcasts of Minneapolis Millers games on WCCO included a large advertising sign board at the ballpark. Though details are sketchy, legend suggests the famous phrase was created as Reeves sketched a box of Wheaties and then wrote "Wheaties – The Breakfast of Champions." Whether it was an agency copywriter, Gale or Knox Reeves himself, the slogan was posted, and an advertising legend was born – marking the Wheaties affiliation with champions.

Ronald "Dutch" Reagan

WHEATIES BASEBALL BROADCASTS were very popular; eventually they were broadcast on 95 stations across the country. One young broadcaster at WHO in Des Moines, Iowa, entered a Wheaties-sponsored broadcaster contest in 1937 and won an all-expense paid trip to Hollywood. While there, play-by-play announcer Ronald "Dutch" Reagan took a screen test. That test led to a movie career and, as they say, the rest is history.

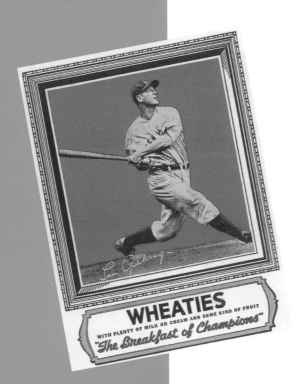

The Breakfast of Champions

In 1934, Wheaties featured Lou Gehrig on the back of the box. It was the first time the cereal package featured an athlete and set an important precedent for the future. For many years, the athletes appeared on the back of the box. In 1958, Olympic pole vaulter Bob Richards was the first athlete to be featured on the front of the Wheaties box.

Over the years, Babe Ruth, Lou Gehrig, Joe DiMaggio, Jackie Robinson, Bob Feller, Hank Greenberg, Stan Musial, Ted Williams, Yogi Berra, Mickey Mantle, Johnny Bench and many other famous athletes have endorsed Wheaties. At one point, 46 of the 51 players selected for the 1939 Major League All-Star Game endorsed the product.

Through the years, Wheaties has had only seven official spokespersons: Bob Richards, Bruce Jenner, Mary Lou Retton, Walter Payton, Chris Evert, Michael Jordan and Tiger Woods.

For the cereal's 75th anniversary, General Mills asked consumers to vote for their favorite Wheaties champions, then re-released those boxes. The top 10 honorees were Michael Jordan, Lou Gehrig, Babe Ruth, Mary Lou Retton, Tiger Woods, Cal Ripkin Jr., Walter Payton, John Elway, Jackie Robinson and the 1980 U.S. Men's Olympic Hockey Team.

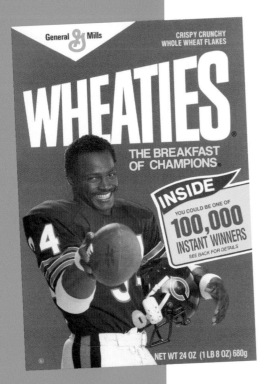

Wheaties Sports Federation

In 1956, President Dwight Eisenhower called the nation to action after a survey found that American children were behind those in Europe in muscular strength and flexibility. More than half of those tested failed at least one of the six tests, while only 8 percent in Europe failed. Working with President Eisenhower's Council of Youth Fitness, General Mills created the Wheaties Sports Federation in 1958.

It was a natural fit. Bob Richards, Olympic pole-vaulting champion and U.S. decathlon champion, was named director of the Wheaties Sports Federation.

Membership was offered to any American who pledged to four basic tenets: adequate exercise, sufficient rest, proper diet and clean living. The Federation also tried to advance the specific goals of Eisenhower's Council.

The Wheaties Sports Federation sponsored many different sporting events and television spots promoting sports and fitness. Wheaties promoted the Federation on packaging by providing consumers with healthy eating tips, exercise information and fun contests.

Down in the valley

The Jolly Green Giant is going strong, considering he's getting up there. The company behind the Giant, originally called the Minnesota Valley Canning Company, celebrated its 100th anniversary in 2003.

In its first year of operation, the Minnesota Valley Canning Company shipped nearly 12,000 cases of white cream-style corn – its only product. In 1907, the company expanded to produce Early June Peas.

From the beginning, the company focused on innovation – spending twice as much on research as the average food company. Several important developments resulted, including new corn seeds that grew taller; more tender kernels that were easier to remove from the cob; and gravity separators that measured peas and divided them into 10 distinct grades.

The company's drive for innovation was so great that in 1932, it had more trial acres of corn hybrids than all the research acres at the nation's colleges combined.

LE SUEUR
Valley of the JOLLY
GREEN GIANT

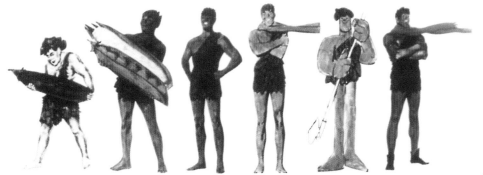

The Green Giant was born in 1925, originally to describe a new, larger, sweeter pea the company had developed. To obtain a trademark for the product, a giant character was created the same year for use on can labels. Ironically, the original Giant was neither green, nor giant. He was white, wore a bearskin and was probably more dwarf than giant. In the late 1930s, the Giant was given a makeover, with a more friendly and approachable persona – this time green. The word "Jolly" was added to his name at the suggestion of advertising legend Leo Burnett.

The Giant appeared in his first television commercial in 1961. In the ads, the Giant called out his famous "Ho Ho Ho." Valley Helpers were created in 1972, including Little Green Sprout.

Over the years, the Jolly Green Giant became one of the most recognizable icons in advertising. He became so popular, in fact, that the company changed its name to the Green Giant Company in 1950.

GREEN GIANT commissioned renowned artist Norman Rockwell in 1938 to create paintings for an advertising campaign to tout the quality, flavor, tenderness and nutritional value of its vegetable line. Rockwell elected to paint corn on the cob instead of peas because, in his opinion, "peas (are) not a romantic subject."

A Cheeri start

The country had corn flakes. The nation was eating its Wheaties. General Mills had even created Kix, a corn puff cereal. And, there was oatmeal. But there were no oat-based ready-to-eat cereals. Until Cheerios – or more accurately, until Cheerioats.

Cheerioats was developed out of General Mills' desire to provide consumers with a "satisfactory, tasty, ready-to-eat oat cereal," according to a 1941 issue of the *Modern Millwheel*, the company's newsletter. More than 500 different formulas were tested and more than 10 shapes and sizes were developed before researchers came up with the perfect combination. "Finally, the laboratory knew it had in Cheerioats the delicate balance of taste and palatability so difficult to find – a tasty, ready-to-eat oat cereal that contained vitamin B1, vitamin G, iron, calcium and phosphorous with added corn flour and tapioca."

A year after the launch, in 1942, Cheeri O'Leary, the Cheerioats mascot, was introduced. Known as "The Cheerioats Girl," Cheeri O'Leary appeared in both advertising and on packaging until 1946.

Four years after its debut, Cheerioats changed its name to Cheerios. The name change was, in part, in response to a competitor lawsuit, which took issue with the word "oats" in the name. According to Walter R. Barry, vice president of Grocery Products operations in 1945, the name was changed to "eliminate confusion which the manufacturers of rolled oats have felt existed among ready-to-eat and other product trade names." The name change, we must admit, has worked out rather well.

Cheerios began sponsoring *The Lone Ranger* television show in 1949. The long-running sponsorship lasted until 1961.

Cheerios ads beginning in 1953 encouraged kids across the nation to connect the "Big G and Little O" to get the "GO" power of Cheerios. In the Cheerios Kid commercials, Sue always got into some sort of trouble. The Cheerios Kid was able to rescue her, after eating a bowl of his favorite Os and feeling the "GO" power. The Cheerios Kid and Sue campaign lasted for nearly two decades.

In 1954, Cheerios became General Mills' top-selling cereal. In 2003, Cheerios was not only General Mills' top cereal, but also the most popular cereal brand family in American grocery stores.

SUE AND THE CHEERIOS KID

All in the family

The Cheerios franchise branched out for the first time in 1979, with the introduction of Honey Nut Cheerios. Its mascot, the Honey Nut Bee, was there from the beginning. The bee buzzed around without a name until 2000, when Kristine Tong, a fifth-grade student from Coolidge, Texas, won a national contest to name the bee, dubbing him "BuzzBee."

Apple Cinnamon Cheerios was introduced in 1988, followed by MultiGrain Cheerios in 1991, and Frosted Cheerios in 1995. Team USA Cheerios was launched with General Mills' sponsorship of Team USA in the 1996 Olympic Games in Atlanta. Team Cheerios arrived on shelves after the Olympics.

In 1999, Cheerios became the first leading cold cereal to be clinically proven to lower cholesterol as part of a healthy, low-fat diet. That important health benefit helped increase Cheerios sales. Honey Nut Cheerios was improved in 2002 to also provide a cholesterol-lowering health benefit.

Combining the great taste of fruit and Cheerios cereal, Berry Burst Cheerios was launched in two varieties in 2003. Berry Burst became General Mills' most successful new product launch in the history of the cereal category.

Approximately one of every 11 boxes sold in the United States in 2003 was part of the Cheerios brand family.

Changing identity

A traditional millwheel formed the nucleus of the first logo for General Mills in 1928. The millwheel logo was used, with slight modifications, for more than 20 years. In 1949, the millwheel logo was imprinted on a flag that became the corporate symbol for seven years. In the mid-1950s, the company developed a new visual identity shaped like a television screen.

The logo changed again in the 1960s because of a successful cereal ad campaign. The campaign's theme centered on "goodness" with every package displaying a handwritten "G" in a white triangle. Within months, the "Big G" became synonymous with both "goodness" and General Mills. As a result, the "Big G" was refined and adapted as the corporate logo in 1963. Variations of this blue "G" represented General Mills throughout the remainder of the 20th century.

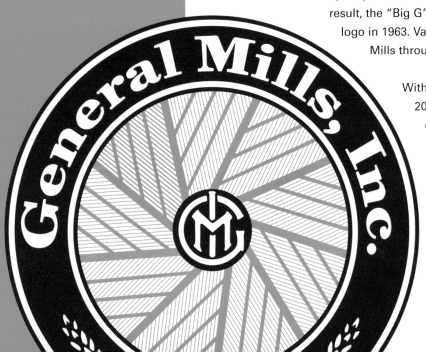

With the acquisition of The Pillsbury Company in 2001, the identity was revised to reflect the combination of the two companies. The familiar "G" symbol changed color, adopting the rich, deep blue from the Pillsbury identity. A series of dots – derived from the Pillsbury "barrelhead" logo – was added to symbolize the continued growth and progress of the General Mills family of brands.

75 years

innovation invention food & fun

ACROSS THE YEARS

GENERAL MILLS

General Mills, Inc.

1928

General Mills incorporates on June 20, 1928. The stock first trades as GIS on the New York Stock Exchange on November 30, 1928.

1929 More mills join the newly formed General Mills, including West Coast's Sperry Flour Company and Detroit-based Larrowe Milling Company.

Our Brands

1930s

1931
Bisquick, a revolutionary baking mix, is developed.

1933
Wheaties "Breakfast of Champions" slogan is created.

1933
Jack Armstrong, The All-American Boy debuts on the radio, sponsored by Wheaties.

1936
The first official portrait of Betty Crocker is released.

1937
Kix, the first ready-to-eat puffed corn cereal, is introduced.

1940s

1941
The Lone Ranger, sponsored by Kix, debuts on radio.

1941
Cheerioats cereal is introduced. The name is changed to Cheerios four years later.

1946
General Mills' test kitchens are renamed "The Betty Crocker Kitchens."

1947
General Mills introduces its first cake mix.

1949
The first Pillsbury Bake-Off Contest is held.

James Ford Bell

1948

Our Businesses

1931
Teaspoon coupon offer marks the first step in the development of the Betty Crocker catalog.

1937
The company divisional structure is established, uniting subsidiary companies.

1934
Research laboratories discover a cost-effective process for producing vitamin D.

1940
The General Mills Mechanical division is organized.

1943
The Mechanical division is recognized with four Army-Navy "E" awards for excellence.

1943
General Mills establishes the Chemical division.

1948
Betty Crocker gave homemakers a recipe for a radically new dessert – Chiffon cake.

Our milling roots

1866 Cadwallader Washburn builds his first flour mill on the banks of the Mississippi River in Minneapolis.

1869 With his father and uncle, Charles Pillsbury enters the flour business, buying an interest in a Minneapolis flour mill.

1872 Charles Pillsbury begins using four "X"s and the Pillsbury's Best trademark on packaging, signifying the high quality of his flour.

1877 Washburn partners with John Crosby to form the Washburn Crosby Company.

1878 Flour dust explosion destroys the Washburn Crosby A mill. A revolutionary new mill is built.

1880 The Washburn Crosby Company wins the gold medal at the first Millers' International Exhibition, inspiring the popular flour's name.

1903 Minnesota Valley Canning Company (later renamed Green Giant Company) is founded.

1904 Washburn Crosby opens a state-of-the-art mill in Buffalo, New York.

1921 Betty Crocker is created as a pen name for answering consumer letters to the Washburn Crosby Company.

1924 The Washburn Crosby company introduces its first ready-to-eat cereal, Whole Wheat Flakes. The name is later changed to Wheaties.

1925 The Green Giant is created to launch a new variety of canned peas.

1926 The Wheaties Quartet debuts what is believed to be the world's first singing radio commercial.

1980s

1983
Kenner introduces Care Bears.

1982
The Olive Garden restaurant first opens.

1983
Fruit Roll-Ups snacks roll out nationally.

1985
Toaster Strudel pastries debut.

1985
Pop Secret popcorn explodes into the marketplace.

1984
Pillsbury introduces Häagen-Dazs ice cream in Japan.

1990s

1992
Pillsbury introduces Shape cookies.

1993
Green Giant introduces Create a Meal! meal starters.

1996
Betty Crocker celebrates her 75th anniversary.

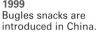

1999
Go-GURT portable yogurt hits grocery stores.

1999
Bugles snacks are introduced in China.

1997
Chex and Chex Mix join General Mills.

2000s

2001
Pillsbury introduces a new line of frozen baked goods.

2001
Milk 'n Cereal Bars enter the market.

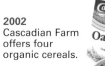

2002
Cascadian Farm offers four organic cereals.

2002
Häagen-Dazs launches Crispy Sandwich in Japan.

2003
Berry Burst Cheerios cereals are introduced.

H.B. Atwater Jr.   1982

Stephen W. Sanger   1995

1985
General Mills spins off its Toy and Fashion divisions.

1988
The Specialty Retailing division is spun off.

1989
Pillsbury is acquired by U.K.-based Grand Metropolitan plc.

Grand Met unveils GrandMe plan for hotels sale
from In

Pillsbury bows to GrandMet at $66

Jolly Green Giant

1990
General Mills establishes Cereal Partners Worldwide, a joint venture with Nestlé.

1995
Pillsbury acquires Pet, Inc., including Old El Paso and Progresso brands.

1992
General Mills establishes Snack Ventures Europe, a joint venture with PepsiCo.

1999
Gardetto's and Lloyd's Barbeque join the General Mills family.

2001
General Mills acquires The Pillsbury Company to create one of the world's largest food companies.

1950s

1950
Betty Crocker introduces her first *Picture Cook Book.*

1951
Pillsbury launches its entry into the refrigerated dough market with the acquisition of Ballard & Ballard.

1955
The first Betty Crocker Search for the All-American Homemaker of Tomorrow scholarship program is held.

e'n Bake Cookies

1957
Pillsbury refrigerated cookie dough is introduced.

1959
The first *Rocky and His Friends* (later called *The Bullwinkle Show*) cartoon airs, sponsored by General Mills.

1960s

1961
Total cereal, fortified with vitamins, is introduced.

1964
Lucky Charms cereal first appears in stores.

1969
Space Food Sticks touch down in the grocery store aisle.

1970s

1965
The Pillsbury Doughboy appears in his first television commercial.

1966
General Mills announces Bugles, one of the company's first snack products.

1971
Hamburger Helper dinner mixes create an entirely new grocery category.

1972
Pillsbury introduces the Bundt cake mix.

1973
Nature Valley granola cereal debuts.

1977
General Mills acquires U.S. licensing rights to Yoplait yogurt.

1977
Kenner, part of General Mills' Toy division, releases *Star Wars* figures.

---

arry A. Bullis   Gerald S. Kennedy   Charles H. Bell   Edwin W. Rawlings   James P. McFarland   E. Robert Kinney

1959   1961   1967   1969   1977

1954
General Mills builds its first Canadian plant.

1953
The Ryan flight recorder is developed in partnership with the University of Minnesota.

1954
The General Mills Foundation is established.

1954
Operation Skyhook balloon reaches a record altitude of 116,700 feet.

1960
The Bellera Air Spun milling process is invented.

1965
General Mills acquires Rainbow Crafts.

1968
General Mills passes go with purchase of game company Parker Brothers.

1961
James Ford Bell Research Center is dedicated.

1967
Pillsbury acquires Burger King restaurants.

1970
General Mills purchases Red Lobster restaurants.

1979
Pillsbury acquires the Green Giant Company.

1975
Totino's is purchased by Pillsbury.

Charmin' characters

General Mills has created some of the most beloved characters in the grocery store. Who hasn't secretly hoped that the Trix Rabbit – this time – will finally taste the Trix?

You wouldn't believe it to look at him, but the Trix Rabbit is more than 40 years old. All those years, in almost every commercial he is foiled by two kids who exclaim, "Silly Rabbit, Trix are for kids!" Through the decades, the Rabbit has actually tasted the Trix twice – in 1976 and 1980 following box top voting campaigns.

Lucky the Leprechaun was born in 1964 proclaiming about Lucky Charms, "'Tis a charmin' cereal ... simply charmin'!" His magically delicious cereal was the first to include marshmallows. In the mid-1970s, Lucky took a short hiatus. He was replaced by Waldo the Wizard, but in less than a year, Lucky "magically" reappeared on boxes. Forty years later, "The kids are after me Lucky Charms," says Lucky with a grin.

Even monsters can be fun at the breakfast table. Count Chocula, Franken Berry and Boo Berry debuted in the early 1970s, followed by Fruit Brute and Yummy Mummy.

Wendell, the friendly baker responsible for cooking up delicious batches of Cinnamon Toast Crunch cereal, began baking in 1987. Wendell's two sidekicks, Bob and Quello, have since retired, and today Wendell works alone.

HE *Goodness* OF TOASTED OATS

Cheerios

THE *Goodness* OF TOASTED WHOLE WHEAT FLAKES

WHEATIES

"Yours for fitness" *Bob Richards*

THE *Goodness* OF FRUIT FLAVOR CORN PUFFS

TRIX

Big new "*G*" on the box means...

THE *Goodness* OF CHOCOLATE FLAVOR CORN PUFFS

cocoa puffs

THE *Goodness* OF SUGAR TOASTED OATS AND WHEAT

JETS

THE *Goodness* OF HIGH PROTEIN FLAKES

hi pro
high protein flakes

very special Goodness from General Mills

General Mills

THE *Goodness* OF CRISPY CORN PUFFS

CORN KiX

THE *Goodness* OF SUGAR CHARGED OATS

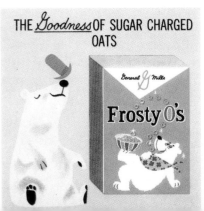

Frosty O's

Goodness IN EVERY PACK YOU PICK

new assortment PICK-A-PACK

'G' stands for goodness

With more than 40 varieties and a leading market share, many consumers think of General Mills first as a cereal company. Today the company is much more, but General Mills is certainly proud of its cereal heritage.

General Mills helped define the ready-to-eat cereal category. Wheaties was introduced in 1924, but marketing innovations like the singing radio commercial are what really helped establish the identity of Wheaties. A few years later, the slogan "Wheaties – The Breakfast of Champions" was coined, and the product was on its way to cereal superstardom.

The company's second cereal – Kix – was the first puffed corn cereal. Introduced in 1937, Kix was enriched with vitamins and minerals, and it was formulated to "stay crisp in cream until the very last spoonful." Today, the Kix tag line "Kid-Tested, Mother-Approved" is almost as well-known as "The Breakfast of Champions."

Four years later, General Mills launched what would become the leading brand in the cereal category – the yellow box familiar everywhere. Originally introduced as Cheerioats, it was the first ready-to-eat oat cereal. In 1945, to solve a

trademark dispute, the name was changed to Cheerios. By 1954, it had become General Mills' top-selling cereal, and it continues to be today.

The company's first entry in the presweetened cereal category was Sugar Jets in 1953. The "space age shapes" were made of oats and wheat.

The first fruit-flavored cereal on the market, Trix, was launched in 1954, followed four years later by Cocoa Puffs, which capitalized on consumers' love of chocolate. Both cereals are well-known for their spokescharacters – the Trix Rabbit and Sonny the Cuckoo Bird.

In 1961, Total was introduced to compete in the health cereal market, fortified with 100 percent of important vitamins and minerals. Lucky Charms was the first cereal to include marshmallows in 1964, popular with kids and leprechauns of all ages.

A popular favorite, Cinnamon Toast Crunch, was introduced in 1984. Chex was acquired in 1997.

Of course, there are many more cereals – too many to mention every one. But cereal remains one of the company's biggest businesses.

Free

Mother: Accept This Brand-New

Jack Armstrong

MYSTERY, "TORPEDO" FLASHLIGHT

for your child, free with purchase of
2 packages of WHEATIES
—*the whole wheat breakfast cereal that
children simply adore*

Out of the box

In the early days, premiums weren't always included inside the package, as they frequently are now. Consumers would have to collect coupons or box tops, and sometimes send a bit of money, to receive their goods.

General Mills issued its first premium – teaspoons – in Gold Medal flour and Wheaties cereal promotions in 1931. The response was huge, and the company quickly moved to leverage the popular promotion vehicle, striving to make each new premium better than the last.

General Mills often used its popular radio shows to announce premium offers. Consumers listening to the shows could then write to the company to receive their promotional items. Then they would spend a few weeks checking the mailbox to see whether their cool new premium had arrived.

Announcements were particularly prevalent on the *Jack Armstrong* radio show, sponsored by Wheaties. At one point, more than six million Jack Armstrong SkyRanger planes were in toy chests across the country.

Through the years, rings have been particularly popular. There have been six-shooter rings, silver bullet rings – and, of course, secret decoder rings. One of the most well-known was the atomic bomb ring in the late 1940s. Consumers could send in a Kix box top and a small amount of money to receive the adjustable ring with a two-piece aluminum and plastic "bomb" – while not an actual weapon of mass destruction, it could be a weapon of mass distraction.

While still popular, premiums have changed with the times. Most cereal premiums today can be found directly in or on the cereal boxes. In 1999, General Mills developed a technique that allows cereal boxes to deliver "visible value," with the premium viewable in a window, so consumers know exactly what they are receiving in the package.

In 2001, several General Mills cereals included limited-edition mini PEZ candy dispensers featuring the Trix Rabbit, Lucky the Leprechaun, Sonny the Cuckoo Bird and BuzzBee. The premiums, the first PEZ had created with cereal characters, were a big hit with children and collectors.

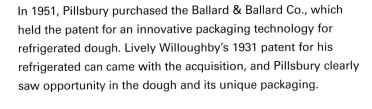

Rolling in dough

In 1951, Pillsbury purchased the Ballard & Ballard Co., which held the patent for an innovative packaging technology for refrigerated dough. Lively Willoughby's 1931 patent for his refrigerated can came with the acquisition, and Pillsbury clearly saw opportunity in the dough and its unique packaging.

Pillsbury asked Ballard employees to list every product they thought was possible using the packaging technology. They came up with a list of about 50 products. Three years later, Pillsbury Quick Cinnamon Rolls hit the market, the first on the list, and Pillsbury has kept innovative new products flowing into the refrigerated grocery aisle for the past five decades.

Pillsbury's other early entries include classics such as Buttermilk Biscuits, Caramel Nut Rolls and Sweetmilk Biscuits. At the same time, Pillsbury created several flavors of refrigerated cookie dough.

Pillsbury created Slice 'n Bake cookies in 1957. Using the innovative new dough technology, no longer did moms have to mix the dough – they just needed to take it out of the refrigerator, slice and place on a baking tray.

In 1961, Pillsbury food scientists discovered a process for manufacturing flaky, layered dough. Orange Danish rolls were the first product to use the new process. Crescent rolls, a longtime popular product, also use the same technology.

Pillsbury launched another innovation in 1992, when the Shape cookies, the "Cookie within a Cookie" arrived in the refrigerated aisle to the delight of kids across the country. Prepared like Slice 'n Bake cookies, this innovative new dough had shapes in the middle of a different color and texture than the outside cookie.

In 2001, Ready To Bake! cookies became the ultimate in conveniece – just place cookies on a tray and bake.

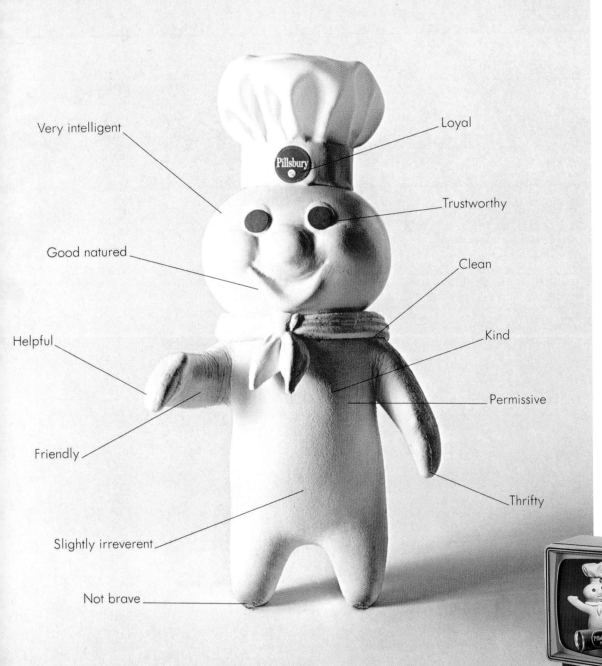

Very intelligent

Good natured

Helpful

Friendly

Slightly irreverent

Not brave

Loyal

Trustworthy

Clean

Kind

Permissive

Thrifty

Poppin' Fresh

The Pillsbury Doughboy was born in Chicago in 1965, but he was raised in Minneapolis.

His first words were "Hi! I'm Poppin' Fresh, the Pillsbury Doughboy," followed by "Nothin' says loving like somethin' from the oven and Pillsbury says it best." Voiceover actor Paul Frees provided the voice and giggle for the first Doughboy (and also the original voice of Boris Badenov in *Rocky and His Friends*).

Recognized as a helper and friend to cooks everywhere, the Doughboy also has a playful side, having been an opera singer, rap artist, rock star, ballet dancer and more.

Created by the Leo Burnett advertising agency, the first Doughboy cost about $16,000 to develop. Five bodies and 15 heads were necessary to make all of the looks and movements for the television advertisements. Using stop-action animation, it took 24 individual shots of the Doughboy for every one second of animated action in each television commercial.

Within two years, the Doughboy was among the most recognized of spokescharacters, known by 87 percent of consumers.

The success of the Doughboy led to the development of a Poppin' Fresh doll, which became one of the fastest-selling toys of 1972. A doughgirl doll, Poppie Fresh, was a companion for a short time.

The Doughboy's popularity has only grown over the years. By 1998, the Doughboy was receiving 200 fan letters and 1,500 requests for autographed photos each week. Poppin' Fresh also has received numerous awards, including "most recognizable and favorite spokescharacter"; favorite food product character; first place in the *Advertising Age* "Whom Do You Love" contest; and "Toy of the Year," according to *Playthings* magazine.

Despite his fame, Poppin' Fresh remains modest and unassuming – even after almost 40 years of superstardom – still blushing easily at words of praise.

Help is on the way

When Hamburger Helper dinner mix launched nationally in 1971, its five flavors – Potato Stroganoff, Hash, Chili Tomato, Beef Noodle and Rice Oriental – revolutionized convenient meal making. For the first time, cooks could prepare a full meal in one skillet, instead of browning meat in one and cooking pasta or potatoes in another.

Hamburger Helper was so popular that General Mills initially had a hard time producing enough to keep up with the demand. It was the right product at the right time. Rising meat prices were stretching budgets, more women were joining the work force – and it was convenient. One pan, one pound, one package, one happy family. Within three years of its launch, four new Hamburger Helper flavors were introduced.

The Hamburger Helper "Helping Hand" made his debut in 1977. His status as a friendly, knowledgeable kitchen assistant contributed to the increase in sales for the brand. The Helping Hand remained in the kitchen until 1996 and was revived in 2001.

Building on the success of Hamburger Helper, General Mills launched Tuna Helper in 1972. Like the hamburger variety, Tuna Helper was popular with consumers. Tuna was the most popular fish in the United States at the time, and Tuna Helper

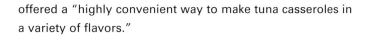

offered a "highly convenient way to make tuna casseroles in a variety of flavors."

The Helper lines continued to expand throughout the 1980s, with the first version of Chicken Helper introduced in 1984. It was not initially as successful as the first two; however, when it was reintroduced 14 years later, it was a hit. Boneless, skinless chicken breasts had since been introduced into grocery stores, and the convenience of readily available, easy-to-prepare chicken made Chicken Helper much simpler and more convenient to make.

General Mills introduced an entirely new line of Helpers – Helper Oven Favorites – in 2000. Unlike the skillet-based meals, Oven Favorites dinner mixes are baked in the oven and allow for even easier preparation.

Today, General Mills markets more than 60 different Helper dinner mixes, so if you need a quick, convenient meal, help is on the way.

WALL STREET JOURNAL editors once theorized that in tough economic times Hamburger Helper sales would rise as a sort of "Hamburger Helper Economic Index." But the analogy didn't hold. Hamburger Helper sales have grown steadily – in good times and bad – more or less since the product's introduction.

Snack flashback

General Mills entered the snack food market in 1964 with the regional introduction of Bugles, Daisy*s and Whistles, and the horn, flower and barrel-shaped snacks quickly took off. In the same year, General Mills added to the company's snack foods lineup, acquiring Dallas-based Morton Foods and its line of "Fun Foods" – potato chips, tortilla chips, corn chips, corn puffs, Twis-Tees and pork skins.

General Mills acquired Tom's Foods in 1966, bringing peanuts, potato chips, baked goods and candy into the fold, and Slim Jim, Inc. in 1967, bringing beef jerky, dry sausage and pickled meat products.

Throughout the late 1960s, the company produced a steady stream of new snack products. Buttons and Bows, Barbecue Vittles, Unicorns, Pizza Spins and Joey Chips are just some of the snacks the company brought to market.

Today, Bugles are still popular, along with longtime favorites Chex Mix and Gardetto's, which joined the General Mills portfolio in 1997 and 1999, respectively.

The introduction of Nature Valley granola bars in 1975 was a departure from the company's established line of salty snacks.

Made from rolled oats and honey, Nature Valley granola bars provide a natural source of energy for consumers' active lifestyles. To reinforce this position, Nature Valley supports and partners with organizations that promote active, outdoor activities such as golfing, skiing and biking, among others.

General Mills created an entirely new snack category with its fruit snack innovation. The concept was simple: deliver nutritious fruit flavor as a snack. Fruit Roll-Ups rolled into the marketplace in 1983. They were followed by Fruit Bars, Fruit Wrinkles, Fruit Shapes, Fruit by the Foot, Fruit Gushers and Fruit String Thing.

After more than two decades, General Mills' fruit snacks business continues to expand with fun fruity edibles such as "Tongue Tattoos" and "Stretchy Faces."

General Mills leveraged its patented microwave susceptor technology to introduce Pop Secret popcorn in 1985. Since then, Pop Secret has evolved into a broad, varied lineup of popular microwavable popcorn snacks.

Today, General Mills has power brands in important subcategories of the fast-growing snacks arena both in the United States and around the world.

Also in the dairy case...

Yogurt has been popular in Europe for generations, but Americans were slower to welcome yogurt into their refrigerators.

Yoplait yogurt was originally developed in 1964 by Sodima, a dairy cooperative in Paris, who brought Yoplait to the United States. Two licensees manufactured and marketed Yoplait in select U.S. markets, attracting the attention of General Mills. Yoplait was distinctive, healthy and naturally delicious. General Mills acquired the U.S. licensing rights to the Yoplait brand from Sodima in 1977. It has since expanded the Yoplait line, adding several types of yogurt and dozens of different flavors appealing to both adults and children.

Yoplait revolutionized the category with Go-GURT in 1999. The first yogurt in a tube, Go-GURT is a fun, portable, convenient way to enjoy yogurt on the go.

Yoplait may be America's best-selling yogurt, but Colombo was America's first. Rose Colombosian made her first batch of yogurt in her kitchen in Andover, Massachusetts, in 1929, using yogurt cultures she brought from Armenia. At the time, the only people in the United States who had heard of yogurt were immigrants like Colombosian. Word of Rose's delicious yogurt – believed to be the first commercial yogurt produced in the United States – spread quickly, and her husband, Sarkis, began using a horse-drawn carriage to deliver her yogurt to customers in northern Massachusetts.

The company remained relatively small until yogurt became popular for its health benefits in the 1960s. Colombo also lays claim to having originated soft-serve frozen yogurt in 1971. General Mills purchased the business and the brand in 1993.

The world's best-selling premium ice cream, Häagen-Dazs began as a small business run by the Mattus family in the Bronx of New York City in 1921. In the 1950s, Reuben Mattus set the goal of producing the "single best ice cream available." He registered the Häagen-Dazs name in 1961 and applied it to his premium ice cream. The name Häagen-Dazs has no real meaning – Mattus made it up, liking the European flavor of it.

Sales grew steadily throughout the 1970s, and Häagen-Dazs was purchased by Pillsbury in 1983. Häagen-Dazs Japan was established as a joint venture with Suntory, a leading Japanese company, and Takanashi, a leading Japanese dairy, in 1984.

In 1999, Pillsbury created an ice cream joint venture with Nestlé in the United States. With General Mills' acquisition of Pillsbury in 2001, Nestlé acquired the venture's licensing rights for Häagen-Dazs in the United States, and for Canada. General Mills markets the Häagen-Dazs brand everywhere else in the world, developing great local flavors such as Green Tea in Japan and Dulce de Leche in Latin America. Companies affiliated with General Mills own and franchise the Häagen-Dazs Shoppes concept in the United States and the rest of the world.

Around the world

William Dunwoody first introduced Washburn Crosby's flour to Europeans more than 125 years ago. By the late 1880s, over one-third of Minneapolis-milled flour was exported, first to the United Kingdom and then to Central and South America. Business was brisk, and General Mills built a mill in Buffalo, New York, in 1904 to meet the demand for exports.

Before the 1950s, international business for both General Mills and Pillsbury was primarily export. In 1954, General Mills began operations in Canada, building a plant in Ontario and introducing Cheerios and Betty Crocker to Canadian consumers. Pillsbury built its own Ontario plant in 1958.

Both companies focused on expansion of their international food businesses during the 1960s. General Mills and Pillsbury expanded flour production into Central and South America. In addition to baking flour, General Mills produced Torti-Ya, a corn flour for tortillas, at its Guatemala mill.

Pillsbury, through a series of acquisitions, expanded its international presence. The company acquired a French food manufacturer, a German canner, an English baking mix firm, a Swiss cookie company and an interest in an Australian baking mix company, as well as flour mills in the Philippines. By the end of the 1960s, General Mills' International division included snack foods in England and continental Europe; consumer foods in Mexico, Canada, Chile, Guatemala, Venezuela and Japan; mineral water in Italy; and soy products in Sweden.

Pillsbury made an important move into Japan in 1984 with its establishment of Häagen-Dazs Japan, a joint venture with two Japanese companies, Suntory and Takanashi Dairy.

In 1990, General Mills joined with Nestlé in a 50-50 joint venture to create Cereal Partners Worldwide to market cereals outside the United States and Canada.

In the 1990s, Pillsbury built wholly owned businesses in key international markets with its largest global brands – Old El Paso, Häagen-Dazs, Pillsbury and Green Giant, while General Mills concentrated on establishing joint venture partners in Europe, South America and Asia. One of the largest of these was Snack Ventures Europe – created in 1992 to merge General Mills' snack businesses with PepsiCo's snack operations in continental Europe.

Pillsbury also acquired important local brands including Latina, the market-leading chilled pasta brand in Australia; Diablitos Underwood, a century-old canned meat spread especially popular in Venezuela; and Wanchai Ferry, a line of Chinese dumplings, to name a few.

Today, General Mills products are sold in more than 100 countries around the world.

Our origins

The General Mills of today has its roots in two mills built on opposite sides of the Mississippi River in Minneapolis, Minnesota. In the 1800s, entrepreneurs flocked to St. Anthony Falls first for the lumber business and later to build flour mills. Cadwallader C. Washburn and Charles Pillsbury were among the first.

Washburn's mill, built in 1866, was originally dubbed "Washburn's Folly." The Washburn mill cost $100,000 to build and had a capacity of "12 run of stone," or 840 barrels of flour a day. Because it was using spring wheat instead of the more popular winter wheat to make flour, most thought that the markets would never absorb all the flour the huge new mill would be able to produce. In those days, winter wheat was preferred because milled spring wheat retained some of its darker bran fragments, resulting in less attractive grayish flour.

Washburn Crosby Mill, circa 1910

But Washburn was an innovator. He installed a new machine called the middlings purifier to remove the bran. Washburn almost immediately began producing high-quality flours that rivaled winter wheat in whiteness and offered superior baking properties. The demand for flour from spring wheat suddenly increased – and "Washburn's Folly" was a success.

Around the same time, Charles Pillsbury began his milling company on the opposite bank of the Mississippi River. Along with his father, George A. Pillsbury, and his uncle, John S. Pillsbury, Charles purchased an interest in an old run-down Minneapolis flour mill in 1869. Although they had no experience with flour milling, the Pillsburys managed to turn a profit the first year.

Both companies grew rapidly in the late 1800s. Washburn built a second, even larger facility in 1874, called the Washburn A mill. Four years later, this new mill was completely destroyed in a massive flour dust explosion that wiped out five other mills and several city blocks. Undeterred, Washburn immediately set about rebuilding the mill, this time outfitting it with revolutionary new steel rollers and exhaust systems that not only made the mill safer, but also produced even higher quality flour.

Businessman John Crosby joined Washburn as a business partner in 1877 – creating the Washburn Crosby Company. That same year, William Hood Dunwoody joined the company as a salesman, traveling to England in an effort to open Europe as an export market for Minnesota flour.

The British were skeptical, as the flour was whiter than what they were used to. But Dunwoody persisted and was eventually successful – the export business for Minneapolis mills grew from a few hundred barrels of flour in 1877 to four million barrels in 1895. In 1879, Dunwoody became a partner in the Washburn Crosby Company.

In 1880, the Washburn Crosby Company entered several grades of its flour in the first International Millers' Exhibition in Cincinnati, Ohio. The company's flours won the gold, silver and bronze medals for quality, and the company subsequently changed the name of its highest-quality flour to Gold Medal – which remains the top-selling flour brand in the United States today.

Meanwhile, the Pillsburys also were building their milling company. To distinguish his product, Charles Pillsbury began adding a fourth "X" to his Pillsbury's Best flour packaging in 1872, adding one more than the three "X" mark typically used by millers to designate their best grade of flour.

In 1881, the Pillsburys completed construction on their new A mill, then the world's largest flour mill. The Pillsbury A mill set a one-day production record on October 12, 1882, when it produced 5,107 barrels of flour.

Innovative thinking at Chas. A. Pillsbury & Co. went beyond flour milling. In 1883, Pillsbury established an employee profit-sharing plan, one of the first of its kind in the country. Originally, all employees with five or more years of service shared in the profits. That eligibility requirement was soon reduced to two years.

The founders of the Washburn Crosby Company both passed away during the decade – Washburn in 1882 and Crosby in 1887 – and in 1888, James Stroud Bell joined the company. He was named president in 1889. Bell, considered the greatest merchant miller of his time, began to expand the Washburn Crosby's presence across the United States.

To drive expansion, Bell assembled a team of intelligent and persistent young businessmen with a wide variety of backgrounds. Rivals referred to the group as Bell's "kindergarten," but there was nothing childish about the men's dedication to the company, or the energy with which they worked to make the business a success.

Washburn Crosby expanded to Buffalo, New York, first with a warehouse in 1893, and then with a mill in 1904. This new mill was instrumental in making Buffalo one of the world's greatest milling centers.

In 1889, the Pillsbury-Washburn Flour Mills Company was created when Chas. A. Pillsbury & Co. and the [W.D.] Washburn Mill Company were merged and purchased by a British syndicate. By 1909, after some financial difficulties, there was a reorganization, and the Pillsbury Flour Mills Company was established.

Around this time, World War I put a strain on the U.S. wheat supply. Strict regulations on wheat flour milling went into effect on Christmas Day 1917. The effect was so adverse that Pillsbury ceased production of Pillsbury's Best flour for the duration of the war.

The market rebounded after the war, and Pillsbury entered the Buffalo market in the early 1920s. By 1923, another reorganization created Pillsbury Flour Mills, Inc., and in 1927, it began trading on the New York Stock Exchange, officially becoming a public company.

The Washburn Crosby Company entered the packaged foods market with a line of products marketed under the Gold Medal name. One was a whole wheat flake cereal that, in 1924, became known as Wheaties.

A change of leadership also occurred during this decade. James Ford Bell, James S. Bell's son, who had been working for the company since 1896, became president in 1925.

In response to a milling downturn in the late 1920s, Washburn Crosby considered dire options, at one point accepting an offer to sell the company. At the last moment, the unnamed buyer withdrew – and James Ford Bell instead launched a bold plan to form a new company by consolidating with several mills across the country. He envisioned a "horizontal integration" of companies with representation from all over the nation, instead of simply consolidating companies in Minneapolis.

Washburn A mill explosion, 1878

Bell saw his vision become a reality in June 1928. He led the formation of General Mills, Inc., consolidating Washburn Crosby and several other regional milling companies to create what would become the largest flour miller in the world. Among the mills consolidated were the Red Star Milling Company of Kansas, the Royal Milling Company of Montana, Kalispell Flour Mills Company and the Rocky Mountain Elevator Company. Other mills joined the new company early in 1929, including the Sperry Flour Company of California, the Kell Group in the Southwest, the El Reno mill of Oklahoma, and the Larrowe Milling Company of Michigan, which allowed entry into the feed business.

Pillsbury A mill, 1890

And General Mills was born.

Washburn: milling visionary

Cadwallader C. Washburn was born on April 22, 1818, one of 10 children of Israel and Martha Washburn. During his life, he would become a congressman, a governor, an army general, a lumberman and a flour miller. He was successful at all of these occupations.

Washburn grew up in Livermore, Maine. His childhood was filled with hard physical farm work, financial insecurity and little formal education. Almost immediately after his 18th birthday, he left Livermore in search of a more fruitful life. Washburn was a man of dreams, full of restless energy constantly propelling him onto bigger projects.

He worked as a teacher, a store clerk and a manager of a survey team. In 1840, he began to study law and two years later was admitted to the bar. He settled in Mineral Point, Wisconsin, about 30 miles from Galena, Illinois, where his brother, Elihu, was practicing law.

In Mineral Point, Washburn formed a law partnership with Cyrus Woodman, an agent of the New England Company. The firm flourished, and in 1852, they established the Mineral Point Bank in Wisconsin. Eventually, Washburn discontinued his law practice and began a successful lumber business with Woodman. Despite their success, the partnership dissolved in 1855.

That same year, Washburn ran successfully for Congress, beginning a 20-year political career. He served 10 years as Wisconsin's representative, leaving Congress in 1861 when the Civil War began. To aid the efforts of the North, Washburn immediately formed the 2nd Wisconsin Cavalry and served as its colonel. Though Washburn had no military training, he learned quickly and served well. At the end of the war in 1865, Washburn held the rank of major general. He returned to Congress from 1867 to 1871, and served as Wisconsin's governor from 1872 to 1874.

During Washburn's illustrious political and military career, he also was playing a major role in developing the milling industry near St. Anthony Falls on the Mississippi River in Minnesota. On an earlier trip to Minnesota, Washburn had been quick to realize the power-generating potential of the 16-foot waterfalls at St. Anthony, and in 1856, the Minneapolis Mill Company was incorporated with Washburn as one of its owners. The company controlled and leased the water power on the west side of the falls.

After the Civil War, Washburn returned to develop his company. He had long dreamed of building a flour mill near the falls, and in 1866, he built the first Washburn mill. It was the largest mill of any kind in Minneapolis, and its capacity was the second largest in the country. Critics dubbed the mill "Washburn's Folly" due to its stunning size and cost.

Washburn's mill was built to produce flour from spring wheat. In those days, winter wheat flour was much more desirable because the harder spring wheat retained some of its darker bran fragments when milled, resulting in less attractive, grayish flour. But with the installation of an innovative new middlings purifier designed to remove these bran fragments, the mill was able to produce whiter, more attractive flour from spring wheat. The flour also offered superior baking properties.

With the success of his first mill, Washburn began construction on a second, much larger mill. The Washburn A mill, completed in 1874, was three times the size of the first mill and, at the time, one of the largest in the world.

On May 2, 1878, disaster struck Washburn and the Minneapolis milling industry as a whole. The huge A mill exploded, taking with it two other mills, causing fires that affected three more mills, a barrel-making business and a lumber yard, and effectively leveling several city blocks.

The initial blast was so powerful that a stone from the A mill crashed through the roof of a house eight blocks away. "As soon as things quit flying through the air, I looked out the front window and saw that the big mill [Washburn A] was gone and the canal was full of stone and stuff," said one witness. "The place where the mill had stood was a mass of flame and the elevator was on fire from top to bottom."

The cause of the explosion was not new to millers. Flour dust had long been known to be a powerful explosive when exposed to the right conditions and circumstances. Prior to the A mill, flour mills tended to be smaller, therefore producing less flour dust. The size and capacity of the A mill meant more flour dust was produced, making it a more dangerous place to work.

More concerned with the loss of lives and jobs than with the destruction of his mill, Washburn immediately set about establishing a fund to provide for the families of the 18 men killed in the explosion. Men who had lost their jobs because of the explosion were given work building the Washburn C mill – which was already under construction at the time of the explosion. Originally planned as an addition to his first mill, which came to be called the B mill, Washburn wisely decided to make it a separate mill.

Washburn also wanted to ensure that an explosion of that magnitude would never happen again. As he began rebuilding a newer and even larger A mill, Washburn searched for ways to make the milling industry safer. With the help of engineer William de la Barre, a safety exhaust system was devised that reduced the chances of explosion by reducing the accumulation of flour dust. Washburn's mills were the first in the country to adopt this safety system on more than an experimental basis.

Washburn wanted to make his new mill more efficient as well, and he had been intrigued for years by rumors of an improved milling method in Hungary. He sent de la Barre to Europe to learn more. The Hungarian millers had stopped using traditional millstones and instead were using steel rollers to grind their wheat. Posing as a mill worker, de la Barre observed and sketched the European design and, returning to Minneapolis, modified the rollers to work in the Minnesota mills. Washburn's new mill was the first in the United States to install these new rollers. The combination of the middlings purifier, the exhaust system and the new steel rollers led to a milling revolution in Minnesota – producing a higher-quality flour than ever before in a much safer work environment.

Washburn was not possessive of his new technologies. He readily shared the innovations with his competitors – ensuring that the entire milling industry would become a safer place to work. "My mills are only a small part of the whole. I can't make all the flour people want, even if I wished to. I have no liking for any dog-in-the-manger business," he once said.

Washburn also made organizational changes to his company. In September 1877, Washburn entered into a partnership with John Crosby and his brother William D. Washburn, forming Washburn Crosby and Company. In 1879, a new partnership was formed when William H. Dunwoody and Charles J. Martin, a Civil War comrade of Washburn's, joined the company as partners.

In 1881, Washburn suffered a debilitating stroke. One year later, the same year that the Minneapolis mills were achieving worldwide prestige and fame, Cadwallader C. Washburn died. He was 64.

The *Northwestern Miller* memorialized Washburn as "generally conceded to have been the most able, active and enterprising" member of the milling trade.

Throughout his life, Washburn made certain that his family, employees and communities were well taken care of. Sometimes it was as simple as widening a sidewalk so that millers could walk side-by-side to work. Other works are more well-known, like the observatory he built at the University of Wisconsin. Washburn's reputation as a generous, philanthropic man was exemplified in his will. In addition to leaving a generous income for his two daughters and his wife, Jeanette, whom he married in 1849, he willed his home, near Madison, to a Catholic sisterhood for use as an educational establishment. Washburn also endowed a public library in La Crosse, Wisconsin, and funded an orphanage in Minneapolis.

Washburn Memorial Orphan Asylum

Pillsbury: flour legacy

When Charles Alfred Pillsbury ventured west to Minnesota in 1869, he had no experience in the flour milling industry. Within 13 years, he would be the owner of one of the largest flour milling companies in the world.

Charles Pillsbury was born in 1842 in Warner, New Hampshire. His father, George A. Pillsbury, was a prominent businessman in Concord, New Hampshire. Charles graduated from Dartmouth College in 1863. Although he was well-liked, one fellow student pointed out that "no one would have selected him as the one member of the class who was to gain a world-wide reputation."

After graduation, Charles went north to Montreal, where he worked as a clerk for Buck, Robertson & Co., a produce commission company. He became a partner in the firm, and worked long hours but, according to an early biographer, the business was not successful. "It is stated by good authority that his business venture in Montreal, before going to Minneapolis, came near being a total failure. When he left that city for Minnesota, all that he had to carry with him was $1,500 in cash and a keenly disciplined business mind."

Most speculate that Charles chose Minneapolis because his uncle, John S. Pillsbury, had established a successful hardware business there, and was a prominent member of the state senate. Shortly after arriving, Charles, along with his father, George, purchased a one-third interest in the failing Minneapolis Flouring Mill. Under the agreement, Charles was responsible for managing the mill.

"Up to that time, Minneapolis flour was way down at the bottom of the heap and the mill had been losing money almost steadily," said Charles. "The other fellows in the business rather pitied me, and said that another poor devil had got caught in the milling business of which he would soon get enough."

When they purchased the mill, it employed seven people and produced approximately 200 to 300 barrels of flour a day. In comparison, at the same time the first Washburn mill was producing 840 barrels a day.

Later in 1869, Pillsbury's uncle John purchased a one-sixth interest in the mill, bringing the family's ownership to half. Under Charles' management, the mill began to operate at a profit within the first year.

On April 12, 1871, Charles purchased the 200-barrel-a-day Alaska mill, with the help of his uncle. He quickly changed its name to Pillsbury and sold a one-third interest to his father – maintaining a three-way partnership in Chas. A. Pillsbury & Co.

Charles continued to build and acquire mills and in 1875, Charles' younger brother, Fred, joined the partnership. By the end of the decade, the capacity of Chas. A. Pillsbury & Co. was about 3,000 barrels a day.

Charles understood the importance of employee loyalty and, in 1883, he initiated one of the first employee profit-sharing plans in the country. Within the first decade, the plan had distributed about $150,000 to Pillsbury employees.

In the company's first 20 years, Charles and his partners had built a dilapidated old mill into one of the world's largest flour producers. They did it by emphasizing quality, efficiency and marketing, and by recognizing good ideas and good people. Business changed for Pillsbury in 1889, however, when the British appeared in Minneapolis.

It was first reported that several British visitors had arrived in Minnesota to investigate the flour mills and waterpower companies on July 4, 1889. Speculation about a sale of the Pillsbury properties continued until October 29, 1889 – when the four owners of Chas. A. Pillsbury & Co. signed a deal with the British to sell their mills to the newly formed Pillsbury-Washburn Flour Mills

Company Ltd. (The Washburn involved was William D., brother of Cadwallader.)

Charles remained at Pillsbury-Washburn as the managing director, and worked there until his death on September 17, 1899.

Three days after his death, the *Northwestern Miller* ran an obituary. "Mr. Pillsbury possessed exceptional executive ability, was keen of perception, and had wonderful capacity for mastering details. Being quick to analyze and to see a point, his decisions were made with electrical promptness, even in most momentous matters, and with a judgment that was seldom at fault.... As an employer, Mr. Pillsbury was generous and considerate, and had a faculty of making those under him feel they had a personal interest in the business.... No man was more loyal to his business representatives than Mr. Pillsbury, and knowledge of this trait filled them with an interest and enthusiasm in their work that contributed in no small way to the success of the company."

George A. Pillsbury

Charles' father, George Pillsbury, was a leading citizen of Concord, New Hampshire. Born in 1816, he was a purchasing agent for the Concord Railroad Corporation for 24 years. George furnished the majority of the money used to purchase interest in the first of Pillsburys' mills, the Minneapolis Flouring Mill, in 1869. He was also president of the Northwestern National Bank beginning in 1880 and the mayor of Minneapolis from 1884 to 1886. He remained a partner in the flour business until his death in 1898.

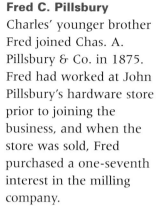

Fred C. Pillsbury

Charles' younger brother Fred joined Chas. A. Pillsbury & Co. in 1875. Fred had worked at John Pillsbury's hardware store prior to joining the business, and when the store was sold, Fred purchased a one-seventh interest in the milling company.

Fred was instrumental in the company's entrance into the feed business. During the mid-1880s, he conducted a series of experiments on bran's effectiveness as a cattle feed. The results were confirmed by studies at the University of Minnesota, and millfeed began to grow as an important commodity associated with the milling industry.

John S. Pillsbury

The first of his family to move from New Hampshire to Minnesota, John Pillsbury was born in 1827. He settled near St. Anthony Falls and opened a hardware store in 1855.

His involvement in flour milling began in 1869, when, along with his brother and nephew, John purchased interest in the Minneapolis Flouring Mill.

John also was very active in government. He became a Minnesota state senator in 1863, and was elected governor of Minnesota in 1876. He served on the board of regents of the University of Minnesota for many years. Under his leadership, the University cleared itself of debt after the Civil War to become the state's preeminent institution of higher education. Today, John S. Pillsbury is regarded as "the father of the University of Minnesota."

He died in 1901.

John Crosby

John Crosby was born in Maine in 1829. Before entering the milling industry, Crosby worked for his father at a paper mill and later for his father-in-law at an iron foundry. Ultimately, it may have been family connections that secured his position with Washburn – he married a sister of Mrs. W.D. Washburn.

Crosby was a well-respected businessman, earning the nickname "Honest John." His devotion to his employees inspired intense loyalty. He served as the president of the Millers' National Association and became known for his frank, no-nonsense character, admired by millers across the nation.

Under his leadership, the Washburn Crosby Company prospered. He died on December 29, 1887, from pneumonia.

William H. Dunwoody

Born in Pennsylvania in 1841, William Hood Dunwoody joined the Washburn Crosby Company as a salesman in 1877. He had come to Minneapolis with extensive experience in the milling industry in 1871.

Hired by John Crosby to introduce spring wheat flour to markets in Europe, Dunwoody was initially opposed by Europeans who mistrusted the whiteness of the midwestern flour. Dunwoody persisted, and eventually persuaded bakers to try the new flour by giving them samples for independent tests. As a result, exports grew from a few hundred barrels in 1877 to four million by 1895.

Dunwoody became a partner of the Washburn Crosby Company in 1879. He died in 1914.

William de la Barre

Born in Vienna, William de la Barre came to the United States in 1866.

De la Barre was responsible for bringing an important new system for the diffusion of millstone dust to the attention of Cadwallader C. Washburn. The exhaust system made mills safer for workers and diminished the risk of explosion by reducing the accumulation of flour dust.

Washburn later sent the young engineer to Hungary to learn more about a new milling method being used there. De la Barre studied, adapted and modified the new process, which used steel rollers to grind wheat instead of traditional millstones, making Washburn's new mill the first in the United States to use this new technology.

De la Barre died in 1936.

James Stroud Bell

Born in Philadelphia in 1847, James S. Bell came naturally to the flour business. His father, Samuel, had been a miller and established a flour commission business, which was the Washburn Crosby flour representative in Pennsylvania where the younger Bell worked. After the death of John Crosby in 1887, Bell moved to Minneapolis in 1888 and was named president of the Washburn Crosby Company in 1889.

During his tenure, Bell saw the building of a new milling complex in Buffalo, New York, and watched the capacity of all Washburn Crosby mills grow from 10,000 to almost 45,000 barrels a day. Bell was considered the greatest merchant miller of his time and believed in encouraging close association of management with employees. He died in 1915.

Bell: corporate innovator

James Ford Bell

The man who created General Mills as the world's largest milling company was a child of the milling industry. James Ford Bell grew up with the Washburn Crosby Company. Born in Philadelphia in 1879, he moved to Minneapolis when his father, James Stroud Bell, became general manager of the Washburn Crosby Company. James Stroud Bell, often called the greatest merchant miller of his time, was named president of the Washburn Crosby Company in 1889.

By the time James Ford Bell was in college, he was actively involved in the company. While majoring in chemistry at the University of Minnesota, he created a laboratory for testing flour in a space over a saloon in downtown Minneapolis. This dedication to science and research would continue throughout his lifetime.

Upon graduation in 1901, Bell plunged into a career at the Washburn Crosby Company. After apprenticing as a millwright, carpenter, electrician, clerk and bill collector, he took a post as a salesman in Michigan. In 1909, he was made a director. After his father's death in 1915, he became a vice president.

During World War I, Herbert Hoover appointed Bell as chairman of the new U.S. Food Administration's milling division. Bell directed operation of the nation's mills during the war. In 1918, he accompanied Hoover on a European relief mission. In appreciation for his services, he was awarded the Belgian Order of the Crown and made a member of the French Legion of Honor.

When Bell became president of the Washburn Crosby Company in 1925, times were tough for millers. Facing dwindling margins and declining per capita consumption, Bell realized that economies of scale could be realized through a consolidation of a national network of mills.

With that in mind, Bell masterminded the formation of General Mills.

In June 1928, the merger of Washburn Crosby and four other mills created the largest milling company in the United States. The new corporation was named General Mills. Later, in 1929, additional mills joined the merger including Sperry, the leading West Coast milling company.

Bell expanded the company's interest beyond the flour business. When General Mills incorporated, it sold only a few consumer products: Gold Medal flour, several specialty flours and Wheaties. Under Bell's leadership, consumer products expanded to include a variety of cereals, mixes and home appliances.

Bell established some of the first, full-fledged research laboratories in the food industry and, in 1930, he recruited Dr. C.H. Bailey – one of the world's leading cereal chemists – to lead the research department. In addition to developing new food products like Cheerios and Kix, the laboratories studied vitamins and introduced an inexpensive process for producing vitamin D. Bell was fond of saying, "Where research leads, the company follows." Bell established a dedication to research that is still at the core of General Mills today, especially at the James Ford Bell Technical Center, the research facility named in his honor.

By the time Bell retired in 1948, almost half of General Mills' sales volume came from non-flour businesses – packaged foods, formula feeds, and chemical and mechanical products.

Throughout his life, Bell was a man of many interests and tremendous personal commitment. When he died in 1961, he left behind a legacy as a businessman, outdoorsman, conservationist and philanthropist. An avid supporter of the arts, he made many contributions to the Minneapolis Institute of Arts. Bell was committed to the University of Minnesota, serving as regent, creating the James Ford Bell Library to house his rare book collection, and enthusiastically supporting the Museum of Natural History (later renamed the James Ford Bell Museum of Natural History).

1930s:
Innovations beyond flour

Food companies prosper as consumers turn to new, convenient packaged food items.

Despite the Great Depression, General Mills made great strides during the 1930s.

General Mills launched two revolutionary products. The first, Bisquick baking mix, was introduced in 1931 to immediate success. Within a year, 95 imitators came to market, but none could displace the original Bisquick. Homemakers quickly realized that the mix could be used for much more than just biscuits, and Biquick eventually developed the slogan "A World of Baking in a Box."

The second product, Kix cereal, was the result of the invention of an innovative new machine – the puffing gun. General Mills had entered the ready-to-eat cereal category a decade before with the introduction of Wheaties. But Kix was very different.

The puffing gun, developed by General Mills engineer and chemist Thomas R. James, expanded cereal dough pellets into different shapes – bubbles in the case of Kix. Launched in 1937, Kix was the first puffed corn cereal on the market. Later the puffing gun would be used to produce Cheerios and Trix, among other cereals.

While the food divisions were busy introducing innovative new products, the Chemical division was expanding rapidly, with substantial research on vitamins. The company began "hitting the vitamin trail," in the words of then-CEO James Ford Bell, when the newly formed General Mills research laboratory discovered that the uncrushed embryo of a wheat kernel was a rich source of vitamins B1 and B2, protein, carbohydrates, iron and phosphorus – a virtual "storehouse of nutrients."

By studying the effects of vitamins on rats, General Mills was able to produce several different products, including wheat-germ oil, and vitamin A and vitamin D concentrates. The division also developed a process for

creating vitamin D cheaply and efficiently, which allowed General Mills to become one of the largest producers of vitamin D in the world.

Toward the end of the decade, in a move to increase efficiency, the board of directors adopted a plan "for the complete liquidation and dissolution of all subsidiary companies." Effectively, General Mills became a centralized company in all aspects, operating all of its mills and associated companies across the nation from one location.

Bell created two distinct divisions within the company. One was responsible for flour and feed, while the other took charge of grocery products. The large feed division sold farm animal products, including turkey feeds, cattle fattener and pig and hog meal. The grocery products division sold flour, Wheaties, Bisquick and Kix.

While the new organization had central headquarters in Minneapolis, executives in the regional locations still had great responsibility for day-to-day operations. Centralization simply gave Minneapolis more overall responsibility for activities such as quality control, mill construction and order processing.

Meanwhile, elsewhere in Minnesota, the Minnesota Valley Canning Company (later the Green Giant Company) was developing vegetable technology that would make it one of the premier vegetable producers in the world.

In 1933, Minnesota Valley Canning began using gravity separators to separate tender young peas from the more mature; tender peas were less dense and therefore floated. The company then combined this process with a tenderometer, which tested the tenderness of a pea, allowing the company to separate peas into 10 distinct grades.

One year later, a company researcher created the "heat unit theory," which improved planting and harvesting techniques. Effectively, it allowed the company to harvest day or night and to program the vegetables to arrive at canneries in an orderly manner. As a result, the slogan "picked at the fleeting moment of perfect flavor" was created.

On the radio

Washburn Crosby Company, the largest predecessor company of General Mills, purchased WLAG, a failing radio station, in 1924. Changing the station's call letters to WCCO, the company's acronym, it began using the new radio station as a vehicle for groundbreaking advertising and promotions. The 50,000-watt clear channel signal reached far and wide, and WCCO became the region's major source of entertainment.

Washburn Crosby's first shows were the *Gold Medal Flour Home Service Talks* and the *Betty Crocker Cooking School of the Air*. The cooking school was an immediate success, expanding to more than a dozen stations in its second year. It joined the young NBC national radio network in 1927 and continued in various formats for 27 more years.

The Wheaties Quartet made its singing debut on WCCO on Christmas Eve in 1926. It is believed to be the first singing advertisement, and is credited for increasing sales with the jingle "Have You Tried Wheaties?"

WCCO was purchased by CBS in 1932, but General Mills continued to be involved in radio advertisements and sponsorships, including Wheaties sports endorsements, which began in 1933. The company's first baseball sponsorship appeared only on WCCO, but Wheaties ads quickly expanded to 95 stations across the country.

Wheaties also sponsored *Jack Armstrong, The All-American Boy,* the first juvenile

adventure serial on radio. The program debuted in 1933 and ran through 1951. In the last few years of its run, the show was called *Armstrong of the SBI* (Scientific Bureau of Investigation). As a tie-in to the cereal, Jack Armstrong would regularly use items that would later appear as premiums offered on Wheaties boxes. The program was inducted into the Radio Hall of Fame in 1989.

Bisquick was responsible for the first radio "soap opera." *Betty and Bob* debuted in 1932 and ran through the end of the decade. The first serial to use melodrama to drive the story, *Betty and Bob* used the central themes of love, hate, jealousy and misunderstanding to tell the story of Betty, a secretary who worked for Bob Drake, the heir to a large fortune. Betty and Bob's world was filled with divorce, murder, betrayal and insanity – daily events that would come to define soap operas. Soap companies would eventually become the principal sponsors of most programs, and unfortunately the name "baking mix operas" just never caught on.

General Mills sponsored nearly 200 shows through the mid-1950s, ranging from serials such as *Dr. Kate* and *Today's Children* to musical programs like *Beat the Band.*

1940s:
Food marches on

American companies rally around the war effort, pitching in and helping out.

After the United States entered World War II in 1941, both General Mills and Pillsbury helped the war effort in several ways. Government contracts had General Mills building military equipment, while Pillsbury developed special packaging to ensure that the troops received fresh, quality food. And both companies made concerted efforts to educate the public on nutrition and efficient food consumption.

By 1941, the General Mills Mechanical division had become well-known as a world-class manufacturer of precision machines and equipment. During the war, it changed its focus to military equipment, developing several important advances. For example, the hedgehog, an instrument that would guide missiles to their target regardless of the target's movements, was credited with playing a significant role in sinking more than 300 German submarines.

At Pillsbury, most of the wartime efforts focused on food and its packaging. Pillsbury developed several products for the U.S. Army Quartermaster Corps, including dehydrated soup mixes. The company also provided food for liberated countries as well as for prisoners of war.

On the home front, both companies provided the public with valuable nutrition and recipe information to help consumers during periods of food rationing. General Mills distributed more than seven million *Your Share* Betty Crocker booklets across the nation, providing easy, nutritional meal ideas that housewives could create using war-rationed foods.

In 1941, President Franklin Roosevelt held a National Nutrition Conference for Defense in part to address concepts of food enrichment. General Mills had launched Vibic flour – enriched with vitamin B, calcium and iron – in 1940. And the Pillsbury Flour Mills Company (renamed Pillsbury Mills, Inc. in 1944) had begun enriching its flour

with vitamins and iron in 1941, giving consumers across the nation easier access to foods containing important nutrients. By 1943, bread was required by law to be enriched with vitamins. Reductions in several nutrition-related illnesses were attributed to the enrichment program, called the "greatest contribution ever made to the program of public health."

Another healthful product introduced during the war years was Cheerioats, the first ready-to-eat oat cereal. Launched in 1941, the name changed to Cheerios in 1945. It also supplied several vitamins and minerals that were the adult requirements at the time.

After the war, both companies returned their focus to nonmilitary products and innovations. Both launched cake mixes in the late 1940s. The General Mills Mechanical division developed a series of consumer appliances in 1946, including the popular Betty Crocker Tru-Heat Iron.

In 1947, a 64-year-old California man approached General Mills with a secret recipe. "I wanted Betty Crocker to give the secret to the women of America," Harry Baker explained. Refined in the Betty Crocker test kitchens, General Mills debuted Chiffon cake. Heralded as the "cake discovery of the decade," and "the first new cake in 100 years," the new Chiffon cake used a secret ingredient – salad oil.

General Mills also developed Brown 'n Serve rolls – a revolutionary technological development in the grocery world. The idea came to Joseph Gregor, a Florida fireman, in 1949. Gregor had rolls in the oven when the fire alarm sounded, so he turned off the oven. Upon returning, he noticed that the half-baked rolls had kept their shape, so he continued baking them. Thus par-baked rolls and biscuits were born. Gregor, a bakery owner, tested the rolls on his customers with great success. A General Mills salesman brought the idea to the company's bakeries research laboratories, which perfected the baking process, and obtained a patent. The patent was then given to the entire baking industry. "What is good for the baking industry is also good for the milling industry," said Leslie Perrin, then-president of General Mills.

The 'General' in the war

The "General" did its part in the war. Like many companies, General Mills adapted its production and products to help with the effort. Food was important, of course, not just for the troops, but also for families stretching war-rationed supplies back home.

The company's Mechanical division played a particularly important role. In the 1940s, the division was known as one of the best precision manufacturers in the world. Its engineers were meticulous about producing machinery with incredible accuracy. The U.S. Army, Navy and Air Force all looked to tap that innovative precision technology with the division being contracted to produce numerous control instruments, various torpedoes and gunsights.

Tom James, a legendary General Mills engineer, took on the difficult task of redesigning the gunsight for the 8-inch gun on Navy warships. For five days, James studied the gunsight and sketched on his drawing board. In those five days, he slept a total of five hours. He continued to work day and night for more than 40 days, sleeping an hour or two each night on a cot in his office or at his desk. In just over one month, he produced an entirely new design for a significantly improved gunsight. It would be put to use months later in the Battle of Iwo Jima.

The Mechanical division ambitiously tackled myriad projects of wide-ranging importance. One project was the jitterbug torpedo. Designed to create a feeling of false security on board the targeted ship, the torpedo would appear to go in the wrong direction, then at the last minute turn at a right angle to hit its mark. The torpedo could even do U-turns and figure 8s in what the Navy called "unusual trajectory patterns."

But the division's most unusual project may have been the training of live pigeons to be bomb pilots. Famed Professor B.F. Skinner trained the pigeons to guide the bombs to their targets, while the Mechanical division built precision guidance equipment to allow a three-pigeon team to tap their way to the target – directing this early "smart bomb" with their beaks. Although "pigeon bombers" never played an actual part in the war, the project remained classified for a decade.

While General Mills was producing military machinery, Pillsbury was assisting the troops by developing special foods and unique packaging to better suit the needs of soldiers. For example, Pillsbury worked with several companies to develop waterproof sacks of food that could be dropped out of enemy range and float to soldiers in need.

Both General Mills and Pillsbury developed products for the Army's K and C rations, including a dry cereal bar – oblong to fit into K rations and disc-shaped to suit the C rations. Also produced were dehydrated green pea and bean soup mixes.

Revolutionary technology

For almost 40 years, the General Mills Mechanical division designed and manufactured a wide range of products, from milling and flour packing equipment to submarines.

The division had its roots in Washburn Crosby Company's Manufacturing Service department, established in 1926 with only six employees. Headed by Helmer Anderson, the department was charged with keeping the flour milling machinery running smoothly. Along the way, the group developed extraordinary capabilities and some revolutionary machinery, such as the Anderson sealer, a machine that glued flour packages closed rather than tying them with string. The Long packer, an innovative machine designed by George Long, filled different size flour bags, automatically knowing when the bag was full.

The division expanded and began working on projects beyond the scope of food, including working with the U.S. Navy. With war looming, government contracts continued to arrive. General Mills' largest mechanical facility was known as a "defense plant," and was part of President Franklin Roosevelt's "Arsenal of Democracy."

Immediately after the Pearl Harbor attack, it became a "war plant," complete with armed guards. General Mills' involvement with the military eventually became so

extensive that nearly 90 percent of the plant's employees were working on war-related projects. Most of the milling-related work was moved to a smaller facility in Iowa. The company's dedication and hard work earned the Mechanical division four U.S. Army-Navy "E" awards for excellence.

After the war, the Mechanical division turned its attention back to nonmilitary work, providing consumer appliances such as irons, toasters and pressure cookers.

In 1947, residents in Minneapolis began reporting strange silvery objects overhead. They were assured they had nothing to worry about, but when the balloons first started appearing, General Mills could not tell the witnesses that its Mechanical division had begun working with the U.S. government on hot air balloon projects. The majority of the flights were to collect information about the upper atmosphere, though some were estimating the spread of potential radioactive fallout in the cold war atomic era.

The balloon department did projects for the Air Force, Office of Naval Research, Atomic Energy Commission and North American Aviation, among others.

Project Strato-Lab, which began in 1946 and continued through the 1950s, yielded valuable information about cosmic rays as well as atmospheric observations not possible from the ground.

By 1963, General Mills decided to once again concentrate on consumer goods and convenience foods, divesting its electronics and mechanical holdings.

The FUTURE is our frontier!

General Mills

Home of General Mills Balloons

PLANT 6

1950s:
Peace and prosperity

The postwar economy booms, as consumers enjoy the many convenient new products seen on TV.

The 1950s was a time of change in the United States. World War II was over, and the country was enjoying the prosperity of a postwar economy. It was a decade of change for Pillsbury and General Mills, too, both domestically and internationally.

In 1951, Pillsbury purchased Ballard & Ballard Co., Inc. Pillsbury's then-CEO Paul Gerot said, "They had one interesting product, Ballard OvenReady biscuits, and a good piece of their profit was coming from this product. If we could build a mix business with a variety of products – pancake and pie crust and cake mix and hot roll mix, and so on – why can't we put research behind this refrigerated idea and develop a wide range of refrigerated products – cinnamon rolls and so on?"

Ballard & Ballard held the patent for a packaging technology for refrigerated dough, which came with the acquisition. Although Ballard hadn't moved its products beyond regional distribution, Gerot saw opportunity.

Gerot asked Ballard employees to list every product they thought was possible using the packaging technology and refrigerated dough. They came to him with a list of about 50 products. Three years later, Pillsbury Quick Cinnamon Rolls hit the market, the first of that list.

Pillsbury was producing 10 different biscuit and roll varieties by 1957. By the end of the decade, refrigerated dough reached profits of $5.6 million.

In 1958, Pillsbury built a food production plant next to its flour mill in Ontario, and several flour mills in Guatemala. In 1960, Pillsbury snatched an opportunity to purchase interest in a mill near Caracas, Venezuela, beginning an international expansion trend that would continue for many years.

General Mills also expanded internationally in the decade, creating General Mills Canada and constructing a facility in Rexdale, Ontario. General Mills Canada launched its first products, Cheerios and Wheaties cereals and Betty Crocker dessert mixes, later that year.

The decade saw continued expansion of General Mills cereal brands, with the company's first presweetened cereal, Sugar Jets, coming in 1953, followed by Trix the next year and Cocoa Puffs in 1958.

The General Mills Appliance division continued to expand in the 1950s as well, with the addition of food mixers, waffle bakers, coffee makers and deep fryer-cookers. The appliance business was sold to Illinois-based McGraw Electric Company in 1954. Revenue from the sale was used to expand the Mechanical division.

Although the Mechanical division began working with high-altitude, lightweight balloons with the Office of Naval Research in the 1940s, its involvement took off in the 1950s. Among the endeavors was "Project Skyhook," which required General Mills to develop a bigger and better plastic balloon that could reach heights of more than 100,000 feet. The purpose of Skyhook was to collect information on phenomena in the upper atmosphere.

On May 17, 1954, a Skyhook balloon reached the record altitude of 116,700 feet – more than 22 miles above the earth's surface. This particular balloon was the largest ever built – 282 feet long when deflated and 200 feet in diameter when inflated. Sent up to study cosmic rays, the huge balloon could be seen at distances of up to 90 miles.

Two General Mills researchers, Keith Lang and Harold "Bud" Froelich, even made it into the Guinness Book of World Records for ascending in an open gondola to 42,150 feet in 1956. They were researching the weight of various papers, wind direction and scatter patterns for leaflet drops.

On the tube

General Mills was truly a television pioneer. In 1939, Wheaties sponsored the first televised commercial sports broadcast, a game between the Cincinnati Reds and the Brooklyn Dodgers. The audience for that inaugural baseball broadcast was the roughly 500 owners of television sets in New York City, with Red Barber providing the commentary.

The Betty Crocker Television Show with Adelaide Hawley

General Mills immediately recognized the potential of the new medium and quickly began using popular radio personalities on television, including the Lone Ranger, and George Burns and Gracie Allen to market General Mills products.

The popularity of the General Mills-sponsored *The Lone Ranger* radio show, which began in 1941, quickly carried over to the new medium. Since he was always on the side of justice, high standards were set for the western hero. George Trendle, who created the character, said, "We try to convey messages that subtly teach patriotism, tolerance, fairness, and respect."

When *The Lone Ranger* first moved to television in 1949, there were only about a million television sets in the United States. By 1952, that number had grown to approximately 16 million. The Lone Ranger, his horse Silver and his faithful companion Tonto appeared regularly on television until 1961.

Following in the footsteps of the popular Betty Crocker radio show, General Mills developed *The Betty Crocker Television Show*, with Adelaide Hawley as Betty Crocker.

Hawley also appeared as Betty Crocker in segments of the *Bride and Groom* television show, giving advice to new homemakers. In 1952, Bisquick, Gold Medal and other brands began sponsoring the show, which also had begun on radio. The show was set in a specially designed studio chapel where viewers would watch a wedding take place.

From the mid-1950s through the 1970s, General Mills and Pillsbury sponsored myriad shows. Pillsbury supported popular programs hosted by Arthur Godfrey and Art Linkletter. General Mills sponsored *Ding Dong School,* featuring real-life preschool teacher Mrs. Frances Horwich, which was a surprise hit. It received fan mail from young children across the country and won a Peabody Television Award for "Outstanding 1952 Children's Program."

One of the most well-known shows sponsored by General Mills featured Rocket J. Squirrel and his sidekick Bullwinkle J. Moose. When *Rocky and His Friends* made its ABC debut on November 19, 1959, audiences watched a moose and squirrel soaring toward earth on a return visit

Box Top Robbery episode from
Rocky and His Friends television show

from the moon. The two residents of Frostbite Falls, Minnesota, had been blasted into outerspace when the quick-rising moose-berry cake they were baking exploded. Subtle, humorous references to General Mills were often woven into the show's plots. In one storyline airing over 12 episodes, Boris Badenov hatched a scheme to counterfeit cereal box tops, since they were "the real basis for the world's monetary system."

In its first season, *Rocky and His Friends* topped the Nielsen ratings for daytime shows. In 1961, it joined NBC's evening lineup. Renamed *The Bullwinkle Show*, the prime-time version was produced in color. New characters were added to the cast, including the lovable, but bumbling Dudley Do-Right of the Canadian Mounties and his nemesis, Snidely Whiplash.

Although the last new Rocky and Bullwinkle episode ran in 1964, the squirrel and his sidekick have never really left the airwaves. Thanks to syndication, new generations of children know the crazy capers of the lovable moose and squirrel and their Cold War counterparts, Boris and Natasha. Adults love Bullwinkle, too – and even today the clever stories appeal to a broad audience.

Sponsorship of television shows diminished in the latter 1950s through the 1960s as television's gain in ratings made sponsorship prohibitively expensive. Most major advertisers – including General Mills and Pillsbury –

turned to spot advertising. General Mills has advertised on some of the era's most popular television shows, including *The Life and Legend of Wyatt Earp, I Love Lucy, The Flintstones, Lost in Space, Dick Van Dyke, The Carol Burnett Show* and many, many more.

Pillsbury aired commercials on *The Ed Sullivan Show* for many years, including that famous episode in February 1964, when the Beatles appeared on U.S. television. An estimated 70 million viewers, more than 40 percent of the homes with TV sets, tuned in. The Beatles rocked America that night with "She Loves You" and "I Want to Hold Your Hand."

General Mills remains one of the biggest advertisers in America, spending millions each year promoting its products, much of it on television.

1960s:
Not just toying around

Society changes, and businesses change, too, diversifying and expanding internationally.

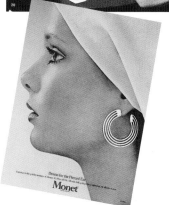

Monet

General Mills welcomed the 1960s by introducing a new method of flour milling. The Bellera Air Spun milling process drastically reduced the amount of time and number of people necessary to mill high-quality flour.

Research on a new flour milling process had begun about 30 years earlier with James Ford Bell's instruction to "simplify" the cumbersome milling process. Bellera, named after James Ford Bell and his son Charles Bell, not only simplified the process, but also milled a higher quality, more uniform flour in one-third less space.

Early in the decade, General Mills dramatically changed its focus from commodity-oriented to consumer-oriented. Within years, the company closed half of its flour mills, exited the feed business and divested its mechanical and electronic holdings – beginning a period of dramatic growth through acquisition.

Between 1961 and 1969, General Mills went on a buying spree, purchasing 37 companies in the United States and abroad – the majority nonfood companies. Although six of those acquisitions were rather quickly divested, General Mills was still a "power to be reckoned with" according to *Financial World* magazine.

During this period, General Mills developed a formidable Toy division, with the acquisition of Rainbow Crafts, makers of Play-Doh modeling compound, in 1965, Kenner Products in 1967, and Parker Brothers, in 1968. General Mills began building its clothing and fashion business with the acquisition of Monocraft Products, maker of Monet jewelry, in 1968 and David Crystal, Inc., maker of Izod and Lacoste shirts, in 1969.

The food business was still central to the company, even during this time of great acquisition. Not only did

Betty Crocker dessert mixes expand with a variety of flavors, but the company began its snack business with a bang, as Bugles, Whistles and Daisy*s were introduced in the middle of the decade. Total and Lucky Charms cereals were created as well.

While General Mills was expanding its operations domestically, Pillsbury was continuing its rapid international growth, acquiring mills in Ghana and Venezuela, and eyeing the European market.

Pillsbury's first European acquisition was Etablissement Gringoire, S.A., with headquarters near Paris. It was an important purchase for Pillsbury, as the 100-year-old Gringoire name was well-respected, and it had several market-leading products.

A year later, Pillsbury made three more European purchases: Paul Erasmi, G.M.B.H., a West German fruit and vegetable canner; H.J. Green & Co., an English baking mix company; and Dorai, S.A., a Swiss cookie company.

Pillsbury also acquired interest in an Australian mix company, as well as flour mills in the Philippines. This rapid expansion added about $40 million to Pillsbury's total sales.

The company also was active on the home front. Pillsbury's most important domestic acquisition was the Burger King Corporation in 1967, its first restaurant acquisition. Pillsbury quickly grew the Florida-based chain from 275 restaurants in 1967, to 489 locations in 1969.

Additionally, Pillsbury developed a low-calorie drink mix called Funny Face. Six flavors of the drink quickly entered the national market in 1969.

1970s:
From yippies to yuppies

Convenience and health gain prominence in grocery aisles as more women enter the work force and baby boomers look for healthier choices.

Consumer demographics were changing dramatically. More women were entering the work force and baby boomers were starting their careers, representing a formidable new consumer base.

To assist busy families, General Mills introduced Hamburger Helper dinner mixes in 1971 in five flavors. Tuna Helper was released the following year.

General Mills rolled out Nature Valley brand granola cereal in 1973. It was the company's first attempt at a 100 percent natural ready-to-eat cereal. The new cereal was touted as healthy and versatile. Advertising pointed out that granola could be eaten as a snack, used as an ice cream topping or as a baking ingredient, as well as a breakfast cereal.

Two years later, Nature Valley granola bars were introduced. The bars were 100 percent natural with no additives or preservatives. General Mills was the first major food company to sell granola bars.

General Mills introduced French-style blended Yoplait yogurt, after licensing the brand from Sodima, a French dairy cooperative in 1977. Sodima had launched the product in France in the early 1960s and had marketed the product regionally in the United States through licensees in the mid-1970s. The product caught the attention of General Mills, and Yoplait USA was created in 1977.

During the late 1970s, Pillsbury divested some of its "toe-hold acquisitions," including a wine business, interest in a Minneapolis housing developer, a flower business and several magazines. The company also made a series of consumer foods acquisitions. Pillsbury acquired Totino's Finer Foods, Inc. in 1975. For several years, Pillsbury had been searching for an avenue to enter the frozen food category. Minneapolis-based Totino's provided the perfect solution. Totino's held the No. 2 position in the frozen pizza category and had yet to expand to the populous East Coast. In 1978, after patenting a "crisp crust," Totino's became the top-selling frozen pizza in the country.

A second important consumer foods acquisition came in 1979, when Pillsbury purchased the Le Sueur, Minnesota-based Green Giant Company. The Jolly Green Giant was as well-known as the Pillsbury Doughboy, and the company had sales of nearly a half-billion dollars. Green Giant was the country's leading producer of canned and frozen vegetables, with a line of frozen entrees in development.

With the emergent use of microwave ovens, both General Mills and Pillsbury helped consumers make use of this new technology. Betty Crocker began a newsletter called "Microwave Memos" in 1976, with directions and recipes for the new appliance. In 1978, Pillsbury introduced microwave popcorn and pancake products.

Outside of the grocery aisle, General Mills expanded into the retail sector, acquiring Eddie Bauer and The Talbots.

General Mills found success in its Toy division when Kenner Products purchased the "galaxy-wide" rights to the *Star Wars* movies in 1977. The *Star Wars* licensing opportunity had been turned down by other leading toy companies, but Bernard Loomis, then president of Kenner, thought the movie had potential. He was right.

The movie was so popular and the demand for toys was so overwhelming, dramatically outstripping supply, that General Mills had to sell "certificates of ownership" assuring children they could purchase the popular toys when they actually made it off the production line.

Something for everyone

Growth through acquisitions has been a key strategy for General Mills throughout its history. In the beginning, General Mills acquired companies that were close to its milling roots. Later, the company branched out, purchasing toy companies, restaurants, clothing companies and more.

In the 1960s, General Mills underwent a dramatic transformation, shifting its focus from commodity-based goods to consumer products. It closed half of its flour mills, exited the feed business and divested its electronic and mechanical businesses.

Then the company went on a bold shopping spree, buying a wide range of consumer products, including toys, furniture and clothing. Rainbow Crafts, maker of Play-Doh modeling compound, was General Mills' first toy company acquisition in 1965. Two years later, the company purchased Kenner Products, gaining a toy box full of popular playthings including the Easy-Bake Oven and Spirograph. The next move was to purchase Parker Brothers in 1968, makers of classic board games including Monopoly, Risk and Clue. The addition of Craft Master Corporation and its subsidiary, Model Products Corporation, added craft kits and Lionel trains to the General Mills family of products.

In the late 1960s, General Mills moved into the fashion business with its purchase of Monet jewelry and its parent company, Monocraft. Soon after, Izod's iconic alligator joined the General Mills family with the purchase of David Crystal. Other David Crystal brands included Lacoste and Haymaker. Later additions to the company's wardrobe included Foot-Joy footwear, with its leading line of golf shoes; Ship 'n Shore, a producer of women's shirts and blouses; and Kimberly Knitwear.

With garment industry experience under its belt, General Mills expanded into the retail sector in the 1970s, acquiring Eddie Bauer and The Talbots. Other retailers soon followed, including LeeWards and Wallpapers To Go.

As the decade progressed, General Mills acquired collectible stamps (H.E. Harris & Co.), a travel agency (Olson-Travelworld) and fine furniture (Kittinger, Pennsylvania House and Dunbar). Pillsbury, too, explored new ventures with the purchase of *Bon Appétit* magazine and Souverain, a California winery.

Because consumers were increasingly dining away from home, both companies made significant investments in restaurant

businesses throughout the 1960s and 1970s. Pillsbury acquired Burger King in 1967. A few years later, General Mills picked up a fledgling chain of seafood restaurants – Red Lobster – and later developed The Olive Garden Italian restaurant concept.

Growth through acquisition was important to both companies' consumer foods businesses as well. General Mills bought snack company Tom's Foods in 1966 and seafood producer Gorton Corporation in 1968. Pillsbury entered the pizza business with its 1975 purchase of Totino's Finer Foods. Green Giant was a big acquisition in 1979, and Häagen-Dazs was scooped up a few years later.

General Mills began the 1980s with a diverse portfolio of consumer-focused businesses. The company consisted of five divisions: Consumer Foods, Fashion, Toys, Restaurants and Specialty Retailing. As the 1980s progressed, the company divested most of these businesses, and by 1990, General Mills had narrowed its focus to two businesses: Consumer Foods and Restaurants.

In 1989, Pillsbury underwent a major change, being purchased by Britain's Grand Metropolitan plc. Under GrandMet, Pillsbury bought Pet, Inc. in the mid 1990s, acquiring important new brands, including Old El Paso and Progresso. When GrandMet merged with British-based Guinness in 1997, Pillsbury became part of the newly formed Diageo plc.

With the spinoff of its restaurant businesses into Darden, Inc., in 1995, General Mills began a new round of acquisitions. The Chex and Chex Mix franchise was purchased from Ralcorp in 1997. Other acquisitions soon followed, including Gardetto's snacks; organic food brands Cascadian Farm and Muir Glen; and Lloyd's Barbeque Company. By the end of the decade, General Mills was positioned to make the largest acquisition in its history – the purchase of Pillsbury.

Major Acquisitions & Divestitures

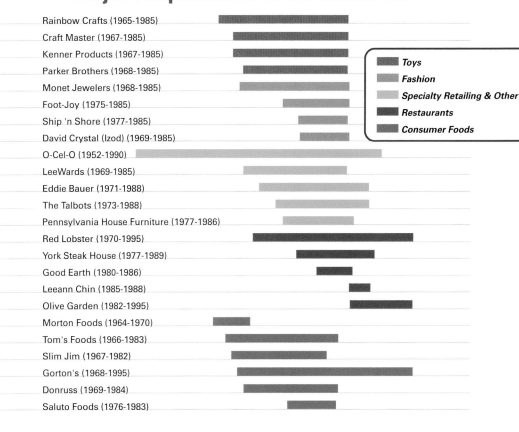

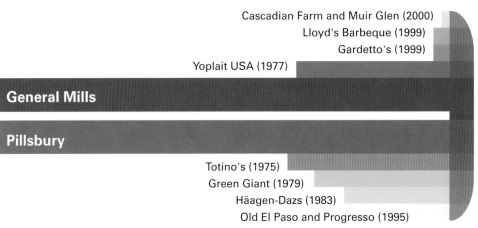

Service with a smile

In the 1960s, both General Mills and Pillsbury ventured into the restaurant business.

Pillsbury purchased Burger King in 1967. Originally founded in 1954, the Florida-based fast food chain consisted of 275 restaurants in 28 states at the time. With the acquisition, Burger King co-founder James McLamore predicted there would be more than 1,250 restaurants and $400 million in annual sales by 1975. Pillsbury did better. By 1975, there were 1,395 stores with total sales of $706 million.

General Mills purchased its first restaurant, Red Lobster Inns of America, in 1970. Then just a three-restaurant operation, the Florida-based seafood chain expanded quickly, adding 350 restaurants in a single decade.

With the success of their first ventures, both companies delved further into the restaurant business. Pillsbury began testing the Poppin Fresh Pie Shop concept in Des Moines, Iowa, in 1969. When it was sold in 1983, its name was changed to Bakers Square. Pillsbury acquired Steak & Ale and Bennigan's to expand its restaurant portfolio.

General Mills developed The Olive Garden restaurant concept on its own in 1982, with the initial restaurant opening in Orlando, Florida. It was one of the first Italian restaurant chains, opening up to 50 new restaurants every year at its peak of growth. At various times, General Mills also owned Leeann Chin, Darryl's, Good Earth, Casa Gallardo, York Steak House and China Coast.

When The Pillsbury Company was purchased by Grand Metropolitan in 1989, Pillsbury's restaurants were separated from consumer foods to operate as a separate division. In 1995, General Mills spun off its restaurant businesses to shareholders as Darden Restaurants, named in honor of William Darden, the founder of Red Lobster. Today, Darden remains a leader in the family dining category, listed on the New York Stock Exchange.

1980s:
When less is more

Conglomerates streamline, returning greater shareholder value through renewed focus.

General Mills was one of the largest toy makers in the world by the beginning of the 1980s. Profit fluctuations in both the toy and clothing divisions, however, led General Mills to make a very important business decision mid-decade. With shareholders in mind, General Mills decided to divest both divisions and concentrate more fully on its main strength – food.

General Mills' focus was solely food when it spun off its Fashion division (as Crystal Brands, Inc.) and its Toy division (as Kenner Parker Toys, Inc.) in 1985, and its Specialty Retailing division, which included shops and mail-order catalogs such as The Talbots and Eddie Bauer, in 1988.

After the divestitures, General Mills consisted of the Consumer Foods division, and the Restaurant division.

Explaining the company's actions, then-CEO Bruce Atwater said, "The companies with the very best results concentrate their resources and their management in a very limited number of businesses which they know well." General Mills owned both Red Lobster and The Olive Garden, and had acquired three more restaurants – Darryl's and Good Earth in the early 1980s and Leeann Chin in 1985.

Yoplait achieved national distribution of its original French-style yogurt in 1982, followed by successful launches of Yoplait Light, Yoplait Custard Style and snack-size packs.

By the mid-1980s, microwaves had proven themselves indispensible in kitchens nationwide. After considerable development, General Mills introduced

Pop Secret popcorn in butter and natural varieties. It quickly built a devoted following.

Similarly, Fruit Roll-Ups fruit snacks made a big impact in the 1980s. The concept expanded into Fruit Bars, Fruit Wrinkles, and shaped fruit snacks, such as The Berry Bears and Shark Bites.

The new salad mix product Suddenly Salad was launched in 1987. It capitalized on consumers' interest in lighter meals and pasta. The unique packaging included a pouch that was used both as a cooking bag and a colander for quick preparation.

Pillsbury made a critical acquisition in 1983. The company purchased New York-based Häagen-Dazs, already established as the premier ice cream brand in the United States. Pillsbury also established Häagen-Dazs Japan, a joint venture with two Japanese companies in 1984.

By the end of the decade, an unsolicited offer was made to purchase The Pillsbury Company. Drawn by the strength of Pillsbury's brands and the scope of its consumer-based businesses, the British company Grand Metropolitan plc, known as GrandMet, approached Pillsbury with an offer. Pillsbury management initially refused, but after GrandMet tendered its offer to Pillsbury shareholders, management negotiated a sale. It was 1989. For the second time in its history, Pillsbury was British-owned.

Under GrandMet, Pillsbury's full-service restaurants, including Bennigan's and Steak & Ale, were sold, and Burger King was separated from the rest of the business. The remaining parts of Pillsbury were organized into four areas: Pillsbury, GrandMet Foodservice, Häagen-Dazs and GrandMet Foods Europe.

1990s:
A world of change

The world becomes smaller, with globalization in the Internet age.

Two important joint ventures were formed to drive General Mills' international growth in the new decade. Cereal Partners Worldwide, a 50-50 joint venture with Nestlé, coupled General Mills' cereal expertise with Nestlé's powerful sales and distribution network to form a new ready-to-eat cereal company outside of North America in 1991.

Snack Ventures Europe combined General Mills' European snack operations, including Smiths Foods and Biscuiterie Nantaise, with those of PepsiCo to form continental Europe's largest snack foods company the following year.

The national launch of Pillsbury's Grands! refrigerated biscuits was extremely successful in 1992. Green Giant frozen Pasta Accents and Create a Meal! meal starters were also popular entries in grocery stores.

General Mills decided to exit the restaurant business in 1995, spinning off its restaurants to shareholders as a separate company. Named Darden Restaurants, Inc., and listed on the New York Stock Exchange, it was a $3.2 billion public company. As the 1995 annual report explained to shareholders, "We believe that highly focused companies with tightly integrated strategies, organization and incentive programs produce the strongest growth performance, so we separated General Mills into two independent companies – one for consumer foods and one for restaurants."

That same year, Pillsbury acquired Pet, Inc., gaining the Progresso and Old El Paso brands. Old El Paso was already a market leader in the Mexican food category, but Progresso was well behind Campbell's in the canned soup category in the United States. Under Pillsbury, the

Progresso brand began gaining – positioning itself with a quality message as the ready-to-eat soup for adults.

General Mills' Cheerios brand was expanding in the 1990s, adding four new varieties: Apple Cinnamon, MultiGrain, Frosted and Team Cheerios. Team USA Cheerios was launched for General Mills' sponsorship of Team USA in the 1996 Olympic Games in Atlanta. Team Cheerios arrived on grocery shelves after the Olympics. In 1999, to help celebrate the new millennium, Cheerios offered a once-in-a-lifetime flavor – Millenios, with brown-sugar sweetened "2"s mixed in with the "O"s.

In December 1997, Grand Metropolitan, Pillsbury's parent company, merged with Guinness, a British spirits company, to form Diageo plc.

General Mills acquired the Chex franchise in 1997, adding both Chex cereal and Chex Mix snacks; then added Gardetto's snacks and Lloyd's Barbeque Company, both in 1999.

The 1999 launch of Go-GURT, yogurt in a tube, offered consumers a nutritious food to eat on the go. Initially, the production of this yogurt couldn't keep pace with the high consumer demand.

Already fortified with vitamins, many Big G cereals strengthened their health profile in the late 1990s. Cheerios, which has been clinically shown to lower cholesterol levels when included as part of a low-fat diet, earned the right to bear the Food and Drug Administration's approved heart healthy claim in 1997. In 1999, calcium was added to several cereal brands. Many Big G cereals, including Cheerios, Wheaties and Whole Grain Total, also qualified to carry the new FDA-authorized claim that whole-grain foods play a role in the fight against heart disease and certain cancers.

Our communities

General Mills and its people have always been committed to helping our communities.

When one of the company's founders, Cadwallader Washburn, died in 1882, he left behind an endowment for an orphanage to serve children "without question or distinction as to age, sex, race, color or religion." John S. Pillsbury was so dedicated to Minnesota that he not only served as governor but also is known as the "father" of the University of Minnesota, its first major benefactor.

The General Mills Foundation was established in 1954. Initially, Foundation grants focused on education, but the focus has expanded to include grants to arts and culture; youth nutrition and fitness; and family life.

General Mills employees are actively involved as volunteers and leaders in their communities. Seventy percent of employees give their time and resources to local agencies. Throughout the United States and Canada, General Mills employees are significant contributors to the United Way, pledging millions of dollars each year to local campaigns. These pledges are matched dollar-for-dollar by the General Mills Foundation.

As a food company, General Mills is strongly committed to feeding the hungry, donating to foodbanks the equivalent of three semi-trailers of food a day.

General Mills has a long history of innovative corporate giving. In the 1970s, General Mills redeveloped the Stevens Court area, an inner-city Minneapolis neighborhood. In the 1980s, the company partnered with the Wilder Foundation and created Altcare to explore alternative health care for seniors. In the 1990s, General Mills lent financial support and technical expertise to Siyeza, a minority-owned food company providing living-wage jobs to inner-city residents.

In the 1990s, General Mills made a long-time commitment to revitalizing a troubled inner-city Minneapolis neighborhood, convening the Hawthorne Huddle, a monthly meeting bringing together community partners to solve livability issues.

In 2002 the General Mills Champions Youth Nutrition and Fitness initiative was launched to help youth improve their nutrition and fitness behavior.

In addition, General Mills brands donate millions of dollars to worthwhile causes annually through programs such as Box Tops for Education and Yoplait's Save Lids to Save Lives.

Washburn Memorial
Orphan Asylum

John S. Pillsbury memorial at
University of Minnesota

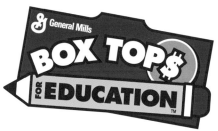

2000s:
Together even better

General Mills gears up for faster growth with its acquisition of Pillsbury – and becomes one of the world's largest food companies.

In the spring of 2000, General Mills CEO Steve Sanger had dinner with Paul Walsh, head of Diageo. Walsh was interested in selling Diageo's food businesses. The late 1990s had been a frenzied period of consolidation within the food industry. Kraft and General Foods merged. PepsiCo bought Quaker. Kellogg's bought Keebler. Companies were looking for product variety and scale.

Sanger saw tremendous opportunity in the potential merger of Pillsbury and General Mills. Both companies had started as flour milling companies on the banks of the Mississippi River. From these milling roots, General Mills had leveraged its grain expertise into breakfast cereals, cake mixes and grain-based snacks, adding other food businesses along the way. Pillsbury had evolved in a different direction, developing unmatched expertise in refrigerated dough products, a strong bakeries and foodservice business and a growing international portfolio. Their individual strengths complemented each other. Each was among America's most respected food companies; together, they could become one of the largest, most respected food companies in the world. Even more importantly, Sanger believed the two companies could grow faster together than either could separately.

A deal was struck, and in July 2000, General Mills announced the most significant event in the company's history since James Ford Bell had united several regional millers to form General Mills. The acquisition of Pillsbury would dramatically increase General Mills' international sales and quadruple its foodservice sales. General Mills would divest Pillsbury desserts and several smaller flour brands, but would substantially increase its presence by adding a variety of categories, from refrigerated dough to frozen foods to ready-to-serve soup, throughout the grocery store.

After months of regulatory review, the company marked its first day as the new General Mills on October 31, 2001. Sanger rang the opening bell at the New York Stock Exchange on November 1, 2001, to mark the first day of trading as the new "blue chip" General Mills. Special "blue chip" cookies were distributed to commemorate the event.

The acquisition was a huge undertaking and had its share of challenges. But the combination has created a stronger company with a record of solid performance.

General Mills in 2003

From a pair of mills on opposite banks of the Mississippi River, General Mills has become one of the largest food companies in the world.

BIG G CEREALS

Big G cereal is a leader in the U.S. ready-to-eat cereal category, marketing Cheerios, the category's largest brand franchise, and other longtime consumer favorites.

MEALS

In delivering convenient dinner options for today's consumers, General Mills is a category leader with Helper dinner mixes and Betty Crocker potatoes. The Meals division also markets family favorites such as Old El Paso Mexican products, Progresso soups, and Green Giant canned and frozen vegetables.

BAKERIES AND FOODSERVICE

With the acquisition of Pillsbury in 2001, General Mills' Bakeries and Foodservice division quadrupled in size. This division markets baking mixes along with unbaked, partially baked and fully baked dough products to leading retail and wholesale bakeries, as well as branded products in nongrocery outlets such as school cafeterias, restaurants and convenience stores.

PILLSBURY USA

Pillsbury leverages its dough expertise in important retail categories. This popular brand is the clear leader in the refrigerated dough category. This division also has a strong presence in the freezer case with its dough products – waffles, breakfast pastries and Totino's pizza and hot snacks.

BAKING PRODUCTS

General Mills has been a leader in the baking category for more than a century, beginning with the introduction of Gold Medal flour in 1880. For busy consumers, General Mills also delivers fast, easy and great-tasting baking solutions with Bisquick baking mix, and Betty Crocker dessert mixes, cookies, biscuits and ready-to-spread frostings.

SNACKS

General Mills holds solid positions in a number of fast-growing U.S. snack categories with a variety of products including brands such as Chex, Fruit Roll-Ups, Bugles, Pop Secret and Nature Valley.

YOPLAIT

General Mills leads the U.S. yogurt category with its Yoplait, Colombo, Trix, Yumsters, Go-GURT, Whips! and Nouriche yogurts in scores of popular flavors.

HEALTH VENTURES

General Mills' Health Ventures include Small Planet Foods, a leading marketer of organic food products under the Cascadian Farm and Muir Glen brands, and 8th Continent, a soy milk joint venture with DuPont.

GENERAL MILLS INTERNATIONAL

You'll find General Mills products around the world, including international mega-brands such as Green Giant, Häagen-Dazs, Old El Paso, Pillsbury and Betty Crocker, as well as leading local market favorites.

JOINT VENTURES

CEREAL PARTNERS WORLDWIDE

Cereal Partners Worldwide is General Mills' 50-50 joint venture with Nestlé. It markets its products in more than 80 markets around the world, including Mexico, France, China and the United Kingdom.

SNACK VENTURES EUROPE

Snack Ventures Europe, General Mills' joint venture with PepsiCo, is continental Europe's No. 1 snack company with top positions in markets across Western Europe.

GENERAL MILLS CANADA

General Mills Canada is among the largest food companies in Canada. The company holds leading market positions in all of its major categories, including ready-to-eat cereal, dinner and baking mixes, and snacks.

HÄAGEN-DAZS

General Mills is a partner in four international Häagen-Dazs ice cream joint ventures, the largest of which is Japan.

INDEX

ACKNOWLEDGEMENTS

We would like to thank the following historical sources:

William C. Edgar, *The Medal of Gold* (The Bellman Company, Minneapolis, 1925)

James Gray, *Business Without Boundaries* (University of Minnesota Press, Minneapolis, 1954)

William J. Powell, *Pillsbury's Best: A Company History from 1869* (The Pillsbury Company, Minneapolis, 1985)

Theodore A. Webb, *Seven Sons: Millionaires and Vagabonds* (Trafford Publishing, Vancouver, 1999)

Memoirs of a Giant: Green Giant Company's First 75 Years 1903-1978 (Green Giant Company, Le Sueur, Minnesota, 1978)